Christmas-Tide

By

Elizabeth Harrison

I.

CHRISTMAS PRESENTS.

Many mothers are sorely perplexed as the Christmas-tide approaches by the problem of how to select such presents for their children as will help them rather than hinder them in their much-needed self-activity. Let the toys be *simple, strong, and durable, that your child may not gain habits of reckless extravagance and destruction* which flimsy toys always engender. Remember a few good toys, like a few good books, are far better than many poor toys. Toys in which the child's own creative power has full play are far better than the finished toys from the French manufacturers. In fact, too complex a toy is like too highly seasoned food, too elaborately written books, too old society, or any other mature thing forced upon the immature mind. Your choice should be based, not so much on *what the toy is, as on what the child can do with it*. The instinctive delight of putting their own thought into their play-things instead of accepting the thought of the manufacturer explains why simple toys are often more pleasing to children than expensive ones.

The following list has been compiled from such toys as have delighted as well as have helped the children of kindergarten-trained mothers.

TOYS FOR CHILDREN FROM ONE TO TWO YEARS OF AGE.

Linen picture-books, rubber animals, cotton-flannel animals, rubber rings, worsted balls, strings of spools, knit dolls, rag dolls, rubber dolls, wooden animals (unpainted), new silver dollars.

The kindergarten materials helpful at this period of the child's development are the soft worsted balls of the first gift. When the child begins to listen to sounds and to attempt to articulate, the sphere, cube, and cylinder of the second gift may be given to him. These two gifts, when rightly used, assist the clear, distinct, and normal growth of the powers of observation and aid the little one in expressing himself, even before he has language at his command. Songs and games illustrative of the various ways in which these gifts can be used with a young child, are to be found in the Kindergarten Guides now published. Some very good ones are included in the first year's course of study for mothers of the Kindergarten College. However, almost any mother can invent plays with them for her child.

TOYS FOR CHILDREN FROM TWO TO FOUR YEARS OF AGE.

> Blocks, dolls, balls uncolored (also six of red, yellow, blue, green, orange, purple), woolly lamb, cradle, chair, picture-book of families of birds, cats, dogs, cows, etc., anchor stone, blocks, furniture for dolls' houses, express cart (iron or steel), spade, rake, or hoe, biscuit-board and rolling-pin, a churn, a wooden case with a six-inch rule and pencil in it, a box of non-poisonous paints—water-color—pair of blunt scissors, paper windmill.

The kindergarten materials found most helpful for this period of the average child's growth are the second gift and the divided cubes of the third gift. With the latter the child can early be trained into habits of *constructive* play, rather than *destructive* play. As all children like to transform and rearrange their toys, this gift is particularly adapted to that purpose. It is simple and easy to handle. Much logical training can be given the child by teaching him to change one form made with his blocks into another, without scattering, or entirely destroying the first form. Many suggestive forms may also be found in the various Kindergarten Guides already published. A series of these are now being prepared by the College for general sale. However, the child himself will oftentimes name the forms made by some name of his own, which should be accepted by the mother. The wooden tablets, sticks, rings, and points of the kindergarten can also be used with a child from three to four years of age though they are, as a rule, less satisfactory than the blocks. The second gift beads furnish an almost exhaustless amusement for some children at this stage of their growth. A long linen shoe-string with a firm knot tied at one end has been found to be the most serviceable kind of a string on which to string the beads. Knowledge of color, form, and number are also incidentally taught the child by these beads.

Low sand tables are an almost endless pleasure to small children, as sand is one of the most easily mastered of the materials of nature, and can serve as a surface for the first efforts at drawing, or can be the beginning of the childish attempts to mold the solid forms about him. When lightly dampened it serves as an excellent substance on which to leave the impress of various objects of interest. In fact, there is scarcely any play in which the sand may not take part. The child should be taught from the very beginning that he must not spill the sand upon the floor nor throw it at any one. In case he violates these laws of neatness and safety, the sand table may be removed for a time.

A blackboard and chalk are usually a source of much keen and innocent enjoyment to three and four year old children, especially if the mother sometimes enters into the making of pictures, or story-telling by means of pictures, no matter how crudely drawn. Various other kindergarten "occupations" may be used by the trained mother—but the untrained mother often finds them confusing and of little use.

Whenever it is possible the back yard should have a sand pile, a load of kindling, and a swing in it, that the child in his instinctive desire to master material, to construct, and to be free, may find these convenient friends to help him in his laudable aspirations. The street has less temptations for children thus provided for.

TOYS FOR CHILDREN FROM THREE TO FIVE YEARS OF AGE.

Blackboard and crayon, building blocks, balls, train of cars, doll and cradle, wooden beads to string, small glass beads to string, rocking-chair, doll's carriage, books with pictures of trade life, flowers, vegetables, etc., tracing cards and paper dolls, toy poultry yard with fences, trees, a woman, and a dozen ducks and chickens.

The more advanced gifts of the kindergarten now interest the child. Clay modeling and paper folding can easily be taught him, and many of the simpler formulas for the mat weaving, also some of the sewing. A good kindergarten is the best play ground for a child at this stage of his development, as he *needs* comrades of his own age and ability. If a kindergarten cannot be had the mother must be as nearly a child herself as she knows how to be. Good, simple, wholesome stories now become a part of the child's life. They form the door by which he is later to be led into the great world of literature. Therefore, story-books may be numbered among the suitable toys for four and five year old children, though stories *told* to the child are better. Almost any mother who has her child's best interests at heart can simplify the old Greek myths as retold by Hawthorne in his "Wonder Book," or the Norse legends as given us by Hamilton Mabie in "Norse Stories," or the rich, pithy experience of the Teutonic peoples as collected in Grimm's "Fairy Tales." All of these contain the seeds of wisdom which the early child races stored away in childish forms, and therefore, they delight the heart of the child of to-day and aid materially in cultivating his imagination in the right way.

TOYS FOR CHILDREN FROM FIVE TO SIX YEARS OF AGE.

Kitchen, laundry and baking sets, balls, building blocks, picture puzzles, dissecting maps, historical story-books, outline picture-books to color with paint or crayon, trumpet, music-box, desk, blackboard, wagon, whip, sled, kite, pipe for soap bubbles, train of cars, carpenter tools, jackstraws, hobby-horses, substantial cook-stove, sand table, skates, rubber boots, broom, Richter's stone blocks, shovel, spade, rake and hoe, marbles, tops, swing and see-saw, strong milk-wagon equipped with cylinder cans, substantial churn, a few bottles filled with water, spices, coffee, sugar, etc., for a drug store.

Ordinarily children of this age still love their kindergarten tools, and can be led to do really pretty work with their mats, folding, pasting, etc. The fifth and sixth gifts [1] now come into use and aid the child in more definite expression of his ideas. More stories should be told, and the beginning made of collections of pictures for scrap-books, also collections of stones, leaves, curios for his own little cabinet. Many references may from time to time be made to the books to be read by and by, which will tell him wonderful things about these treasures. In this way a desire to learn to read is awakened, and soon the world of nature and of books takes the place of toys, except of course, those by means of which bodily skill is gained and tested. These later belong in general to the period of boyhood and girlhood.

To this list of Christmas toys is added a list of books suitable for Christmas gifts. Very handsome books are to be avoided, as the child delights in handling his own books almost as much as his own toys. The value of the right kind of books cannot be too much emphasized. Is not the food which you give to your child's mind of as much importance as that which you give to his body?

When your boy stops questioning you, he has not stopped questioning concerning life and its problems; he has turned to those silent companions which you have placed upon his bookshelf or on the library table. Shall heroes and prophets be his counselors, or shall "Peck's Bad Boy" and the villain of the dime novel teach him how to look at life? *It rests with you.*

There is a great difference between books which are to be read *to* children, those which are to be read *with* children, and those which are to be read *by* children.

II.

THE PLACE OF TOYS IN THE EDUCATION OF A CHILD.

As Christmas is peculiarly the season for toy-giving and toy-receiving, it may be well for the mother to consider this subject.

Old Homer, back in the past ages, shows us a charming picture of Nausicaa and her maidens, after a hard day's washing, resting themselves with a game of ball. Thus we see this most free and graceful plaything connected with that free and beautifully developed nation which has been the admiration of the world ever since. Plato has said, "The plays of children have the mightiest influence on the maintenance or non-maintenance of laws"; and again, "During earliest childhood, the soul of the nursling should be made cheerful and kind, by keeping away from him sorrow and fear and pain, by soothing him with sound of the pipe and of rhythmical movement." He still further advised that the children should be brought to the temples, and allowed to play under the supervision of nurses, presumably trained for that purpose. Here we see plainly foreshadowed the Kindergarten, whose foundation is "education by play"; as the study of the Kindergarten system leads to the earnest, thoughtful consideration of the office of play, and the exact value which the plaything or toy has in the development of the child, when this is once understood, the choice of what toys to give to children is easily made.

In the world of nature, we find the blossom comes before the fruit; in history, art arose long before science was possible; in the human race, the emotions are developed sooner than the reason. With the individual child it is the same; the childish heart opens spontaneously in play, the barriers are down, and the loving mother or the wise teacher can find entrance into the inner court as in no other way. The child's *sympathies* can be attracted towards an object, person, or line of conduct much earlier than his reason can grasp any one of them. His emotional nature can and does receive impressions long before his intellectual nature is ready for them; in other words, he can *love* before he can *understand*.

One of the mistakes of our age is, that we begin by educating our children's *intellects* rather than their *emotions*. We leave these all-powerful factors, which give to life its coloring of light or darkness, to the oftentimes insufficient training of the ordinary family life—insufficient, owing to its thousand interruptions and pre-occupations. The results are, that many children grow up cold, hard, matter-of-fact, with little of poetry, sympathy, or ideality to enrich their lives—mere Gradgrinds in God's world of beauty. We starve the healthful emotions of children in order that we may overfeed their intellects. Is not this doing them a great wrong? When the sneering tone is heard, and the question "Will it pay?" is the all-important one, do we not see the result of such training? Possibly the unwise training of the emotional nature may give it undue preponderance, producing morbid sentimentalists, who think that the New Testament would be greatly improved if the account of Christ driving the money-changers from the temple, or his denunciation of the Pharisees, could be omitted. Such people feed every able-bodied tramp brought by chance to their doors, and yet make no effort to lighten the burden of the poor sewing-woman of our great cities, who is working at almost starvation prices. This is a minor danger, however. The education of the heart must advance along with that of the head, if well-balanced character is to be developed.

Pedagogy tells us that "*the science of education is the science of interesting*"; and yet, but few pedagogues have realized the importance of *educating the interest of the child*. In other words, little or no value has been attached to the likes and dislikes of children; but in reality they are very important.

A child can be given any quantity of information, he can be made to get his lessons, he can even be crowded through a series of examinations, but that is not *educating* him. Unless his interest in the subject has been awakened, the process has been a failure. *Once get him thoroughly interested and he can educate himself, along that line, at least.*

Hence the value of toys; they are not only promoters of play, but they appeal to the sympathies and give exercise to the emotions; in this way a hold is gotten upon the child, by interesting him before more intellectual training can make much impression. The two next great obstacles to the exercise of the right emotions are *fear* and *pity*; these do not come into the toy-world, hence we can see how toys, according to their own tendencies, help in the healthful education of the child's emotions, through his emotions the education of his thoughts, through his thoughts the education of his will, and hence his character. One can readily see how this is so. By means of their dolls, wagons, drums, or other toys, children's thoughts are turned in certain directions. They play that they are mothers and fathers, or shop-keepers, or soldiers, as the case may be. Through their dramatic play, they become interested more and more in those phases of life which they have imitated, and that which they watch and imitate they become like.

The toy-shops of any great city are to him who can read the signs of the times, prophecies of the future of that city. They not only predict the future career of a people, but they tell us of national tendencies. Seguin, in his report on the educational exhibit at Vienna a few years ago, said: "The nations which had the most toys had, too, more individuality, ideality, and heroism." And again: "The nations which have been made famous by their artists, artisans, and idealists supplied their infants with toys." It needs but a moment's thought to recognize the truth of this statement. Children who have toys exercise their *own* imagination, put into action their *own ideals*. Ah me, how much that means! What ideals have been strangled in the breasts of most of us because others did not think as we did! With the toy, an outline only is drawn; the child must fill in the details. On the other hand, in story-books the details are given. Both kinds of training are needed: individual development, and participation in the development of others—of the world, of the past, of the *All*. With this thought of the influence of toys upon the life of nations, a visit to any large toy-shop becomes an interesting and curious study. The following is the testimony, unconsciously given, by the shelves and counters in one of the large importing establishments which gather together and send out the playthings of the world. The *French* toys include nearly all the pewter soldiers, all guns and swords; surely, such would be the toys of the nation which produced a Napoleon. All Punch and Judy shows are of French manufacture; almost all miniature theaters; all doll tea-sets which have wine-glasses and finger-bowls attached. The French *dolls* mirror the fashionable world, with all its finery and unneeded luxury, and hand it down to the little child. No wonder Frances Willard made a protest against dolls, if she had in mind the *French* doll.

"You see," said the guileless saleswoman, as she handed me first one and then another of these dolls, thinking doubtless that she had a slow purchaser whom she had to assist in making a selection, "you can dress one of these dolls as a lady, or as a little girl, just as you like." And sure enough, the very baby dolls had upon their faces the smile of the society flirt, or the deep, passionate look of the woman who had seen the world. I beheld the French Salons of the eighteenth century still lingering in the nineteenth-century dolls. All their toys are dainty, artistic, exquisitely put together, but lack strength and power of endurance, are low or shallow in aim, and are oftentimes inappropriate in the extreme. For instance, I was shown a Noah's Ark with a rose-window of stained glass in one end of it. Do we not see the same thing in French literature? Racine's Orestes, bowing and complimenting his Iphigenia, is the same French adornment of the strong, simple, Greek story that the pretty window was of the Hebrew Ark.

The *German* toys take another tone. They are heavier, stronger, and not so artistic, and largely represent the home and the more primitive forms of trade-life. From Germany we get all our ready-made doll-houses, with their clean tile floors and clumsy porcelain stoves, their parlors with round iron center-tables, and stiff, ugly chairs with the inevitable lace tidies. Here and there in these miniature houses we see a tiny pot of artificial flowers. All such playthings tend to draw the child's thoughts to the home life. Next come the countless number of toy butcher shops, bakers, blacksmiths, and other representations of the small, thrifty, healthful trade-life which one sees all over Germany. Nor is the child's love attracted toward the home and the shops alone. Almost all of the better class of toy horses and carts are of German manufacture. The "woolly sheep," so dear to childish heart, is of the same origin. Thus a love for simple, wholesome out-of-door activities is instilled.

And then the German dolls! One would know from the dolls alone that Germany was the land of Froebel and the birthplace of the Kindergarten, that it was the country where even the beer-gardens are softened and refined by the family presence. All the regulation ornaments for Christmas trees come from this nation, bringing with them memories of Luther; of his breaking away from the celibacy enjoined by the church; of his entering into the joyous family life, and trying to bring with him into the home life all that was sacred in the church—Christmas festivals along with the rest. Very few firearms come from this nation, but among them I saw some strong cast-iron cannons from Berlin; they looked as if Bismarck himself might have ordered their manufacture.

The *Swiss* toys are largely the bluntly carved wooden cattle, sheep and goats, with equally blunt shepherds and shepherdesses, reminding one forcibly of the dull faces of those much-enduring beasts of burden called Swiss peasants. I once saw a Swiss girl who had sold to an American woman, for a few francs, three handkerchiefs, the embroidering of which had occupied the evenings of her entire winter; there was no look of discontent or disgust as the American tossed them into her trunk with a lot of other trinkets, utterly oblivious of the amount of human life which had been patiently worked into them. What kind of toys could come from a people among whom such scenes are accepted as a matter of course?

The *English* rag doll is particularly national in its placidity of countenance. The British people stand pre-eminent in the matter of story-books for children, but, so far as I have been able to observe, are somewhat lacking in originality as to toys; possibly this is due to the out-of-door life encouraged among them.

When I asked to see the *American* toys, my guide turned, and with a sweep of her hand, said: "These *trunks* are American. All doll-trunks are manufactured in this country." Surely our Emerson was right when he said that "the tape-worm of travel was in every American." Here we see the beginning of the restless, migratory spirit of our people; even these children's toys suggest, "How nice it would be to pack up and go somewhere!" All tool-chests are of domestic origin. Seemingly, all the inventions of the Yankee mind are reproduced in miniature form to stimulate the young genius of our country.

The *Japanese* and *Chinese* toys are a curious study, telling of national traits as clearly as do their laws or their religion. They are endurable, made to last unchanged a long time; no flimsy tinsel is used which can be admired for the hour, then cast aside. If "the hand of Confucius reaches down through twenty-four centuries of time still governing his people," so, too, can the carved ivory or inlaid wooden toy be used without injury or change by at least one or two successive generations of children.

Let us turn to the study of the development of the race as a whole, that we may the better grasp this thought. The toy not only directs the emotional activity of the child, but also forms a bridge between the great realities of life and his small capacities. To man was given the dominion over the earth, but it was a potential dominion. He had to conquer the beasts of the field; to develop the resources of the earth; by his *own effort* to subordinate all things else unto himself. We see the faint foreshadowing, or presentiment, of this in the myths and legends of the race. The famous wooden horse of Troy, accounts of which have come down to us in a dozen different channels of literature and history, seems to have been the forerunner of the nineteenth-century bomb, which defies walls and leaps into the enemy's camp, scattering death and destruction in every direction. At least, the two have the same effect; they speedily put an end to physical resistance, and bring about consultation and settlement by arbitration. The labors of Hercules tell the same story in another form—man's power to make nature perform the labors appointed to him; the winged sandals of Hermes, Perseus' cloak of invisibility, the armor of Achilles, and a hundred other charming myths, all tell us of man's sense of his sovereignty over nature. The old Oriental stories of the enchanted carpet tell us that the sultan and his court had but to step upon it, ere it rose majestically and sailed unimpeded through the air, and landed its precious freight at the desired destination. Is not this the dim feeling in the breasts of the childish race that *man* ought to have power to transcend space, and by his intelligence contrive to convey himself from place to place? Are not our luxurious palace cars almost fulfilling these early dreams? What are the fairy tales of the Teutonic people, which Grimm has so laboriously collected for us? They have lived through centuries of time, because they have told of genii and giant, governed by the will of puny man and made to do his bidding. Eagerly the race has read them, pleased to see symbolically pictured forth man's power over elements stronger than himself. In fact, the study of the race development is much like the study of those huge, almost obliterated outlines upon the walls of Egyptian temples—dim, vague, fragmentary, yet giving us glimpses of insight and flashes of light, which aid much in the understanding of the meaning of to-day. We find the instincts of the race renewed in each new-born infant. Each individual child desires to master his surroundings. He cannot yet drive a real horse and wagon, but his very soul delights in the three-inch horse and the gayly painted wagon attached; he cannot tame real tigers and lions, but his eyes dance with pleasure as he places and replaces the animals of his toy menagerie; he cannot at present run engines or direct railways, but he can control for a whole half-hour the movement of his miniature train; he is not yet ready for real fatherhood, but he can pet and play with, and rock to sleep, and tenderly guard the doll baby.

Dr. Seguin also calls attention to the fact that a handsomely dressed lady will be passed by unnoticed by a child, whereas her counterpart in a foot-long doll will call forth his most rapt attention; the one is too much for the small brain, the other is just enough.

The boy who has a toy gun marches and drills and camps and fights many a battle before the real battle comes. The little girl who has a toy stove plays at building a fire and putting on a kettle long before these real responsibilities come to her.

A young mother, whose daughter had been for some time in a Kindergarten, came to me and said, "I have been surprised to see how my little Katherine handles the baby, and how sweetly and gently she talks to him." I said to the daughter, "Katherine, where did you learn how to talk to baby, and to take care of one so nicely?" "Why, that's the way we talk to the dolly at Kindergarten!" she replied. Her powers of baby-loving had been developed definitely by the toy baby, so that when the real baby came, she was ready to transfer her tenderness to the larger sphere. Thus, as I said before, toys form a bridge between the great realities and possibilities of life, and the small capacities of the child. If wisely selected, they lead him on from conquering yet to conquer. Thus he enters ever widening and increasing fields of activity, until he stands as God intended he should stand, the master of all the elements and forces about him, until he can bid the solid earth, "Bring forth thy treasures"; until he can say unto the great ocean, "Thus far shalt thou go and no farther"; until he can call unto the quick lightning, "Speak thou my words across a continent"; until he can command the fierce fire, "Do thou my bidding"; and earth, and air, and fire, and water, become the servants of the divine intelligence which is within him.

III.

HOW TO CELEBRATE CHRISTMAS.

SUGGESTIONS FOR MOTHERS AND KINDERGARTNERS.

All festival occasions, when rightly used, have a unifying effect upon the family, neighborhood, Sunday-school, church, state, or nation, in that they direct all minds, for the time being, away from self, and in one direction, toward one central thought. The family festivals are an enormous power in the hands of the mother who knows how to use them aright. By means of the birthday anniversaries, Fourth of July, Thanksgiving, and above all, Christmas, she can direct her children's activities into channels of unselfish endeavor.

Of all festivals of the year the Christmas festival is perhaps the least understood, that is, if one is to judge by the manner in which the day is generally observed. *Why do we celebrate Christmas? What are we celebrating?* Is it not the greatest manifestation of love, unselfish love, that has ever been revealed to man? And how, as a rule, are children taught to observe it? Usually by expecting an undue amount of attention, an unlimited amount of injudicious feeding, and a selfish exaction of unneeded presents; thus egotism, greed, and selfishness are fostered, where love, generosity, and self-denial should be exercised.

The Christmas season is the season in which *the joy of giving* should be so much greater than that of receiving, that the child, through his own experiences, is prepared somewhat to comprehend that great truth, "God so loved the world that he gave his only begotten Son."

For weeks beforehand the mother can lay her plans by means of which each child in the family may be led to make something, or may do without something, or may earn money for the purchase of something, which is to add to his Christmas joy by enabling him to give to those he loves, and also to some less fortunate child who, but for his thoughtfulness, would be without any Christmas "cheer." In this endeavor, of course, the mother must join with heart and soul, else the giving is liable to become a mere formal fulfillment of a taxing obligation.

Little children, when rightly dealt with, enjoy putting *themselves* into the preparations with which they are to surprise and please others fully as much, if not more, than they enjoy receiving presents. So near as yet are they to the hand of God that unselfish love is an easy thing to inculcate. Let me contrast two preparations for Christmas which have passed under my own eye. In the first case I chanced to be in one of those crowded toy-shops where hurried, tired women are trying to fill out their lists of supposed obligations for the Christmas season. All was confusion and haste, impatience, and more or less ill-humor. My attention was directed towards a handsomely dressed mother, leading by the hand an over-dressed little girl of about eight years of age. The tones of the woman's voice struck like a discord through my soul. "Come on!" said she petulantly to the child who had stopped for a moment to admire some new toy. "Come on, we have to give her something and we may as well buy her a couple of dolls. They'll be broken to pieces in three weeks' time, but that's no matter to us. Come on, I've no time to wait." This last was accompanied by an impatient jerk of the loitering child's arm. Thus what *should have been the joy of Christmas-giving was made to that child a disagreeable, unwilling and useless expenditure of money*. What part of the real Christmas spirit, the God spirit "which so loved the world," could possibly come to a child from such a preparation for Christmas as this? Nor is it an unusual occurrence. Go into any of our large stores and shops just before Christmas and you will see scores of women checking off their lists in a way which shows the relief of having "one more present settled." All the great, true, and beautiful spirit of Christmas joy is gone and a mere commercial transaction, oftentimes a vulgar display of wealth, has taken its place.

On the other hand, go with me into one of our quiet Kindergartens, where the sunshine without is rivaled by the sunshine within. See the white-aproned teacher seat herself and gather around her the group of eager children. Listen to the tones of her voice when she says, "Oh, children, children! You don't know what a happy time I am going to let you have this Christmas! Just guess, each one of you, what we are going to do to make this the gladdest, brightest, happiest Christmas that ever was!" Look into the eager little faces anticipating a new joy, knowing from past experience that the joy means effort, endeavor, self-control, and self-denial; nevertheless, that it means happiness too. Listen to the eager questions and plans of the children. Some of them, alas, are showing their past training in selfishness, by their "You're going to give each of us a present," or "You're going to have a party!" Then hear her gleeful answer, "No, guess again, it is better than that!—better even than that!" Then, after a pause, during which expectation stands on tiptoe, "I am going to let each one of you be a little Santa Claus. We are going to make not only mamma and papa happy, but also some dear little child who might not have a happy Christmas unless we gave one to him!" Listen, as I have listened, to the clapping of hands after such an announcement. Look at the light which comes into the eyes. Notice the eager look of interest upon each childish face as all seat themselves at the work-table and the plan of work is more definitely laid out. Go, as I have gone, morning after morning, and see these same children working patiently, earnestly, and continuously upon the little gifts which are to make Christmas happier for some one else. Will you then need to ask the question as to which is the truer way of celebrating the holy Christmas time? Not that I would have any mother deprived of the pleasure of giving to her children, any more than I would have her children robbed of their pleasure of giving to others. Let us be careful that our gifts are not gifts of useless profusion, of such articles as cultivate self-indulgence, vanity, or indolence. Gifts for children should be few and simple, such as are suggestive and will aid them in the future drawing out of their own inner thoughts or ideals. Above all let the joy of having given of his best to some one else be the chief thought of the glad Christmas time.

IV.

SANTA CLAUS.

All little children are poets if not marred by the prosaic parent or teacher who unintentionally dulls the imaginative faculties by insisting upon their minds dwelling exclusively on *facts* which can be verified by the five senses.

Much innocent pleasure as well as much development of intellectual power is lost by this misapprehension of a child's needs. *All great truth must come to the immature mind in an embodied form* or by means of a symbol. In fact, we of more mature culture still cling to the sacred symbols of the church by means of which communion with the Divine and the regenerating power of the spirit of God are expressed. The spire of a church, the flag of our nation, the medal with which we decorate the breast of a hero, are but a few of the symbols with which we are all familiar. Indeed, if symbols were banished from our daily lives much of pleasure and beauty would be lost.

Again, when we insist upon mere facts being presented to our children we rob them of the great heirloom which has come down to them from the past in the form of those inexhaustible mythical stories by means of which the race has learned its most beautiful lessons of the true nobility and grandeur of life; stories so rich and full and significant that two or three thousand years have not dimmed their luster, nor lessened their power to hold and impress the childish mind.

As the Christmas season approaches many honest, earnest parents are perplexed as to what to do with the time-honored legend of Santa Claus. They do not realize that he is but the poetic embodiment of the Christian thought of great love manifesting itself through giving. The joyous loving nature of the innocent Santa Claus brings closer to the childish heart the realization of the willingness with which the Divine Father gave to his children—mankind. The traditional fireplace through which the beloved Santa Claus gains entrance into the house is but a symbol of that center of light and warmth and cheer which love lights in every true home. The mystery of the coming and going of this great-hearted lover of good little children is but the embodied way of expressing that mystery of love which makes labor light and sacrifice a pleasure. The whole legend of Santa Claus, when rightly understood, is but the necessarily crude—and therefore more easily grasped—foreshadowing of the sacred thought of God's infinite love which lies at the very center of the Christmas thought. No one can deplore more than we Kindergartners do the coarse and oftentimes grotesque representations of Santa Claus which are to be seen in many advertisements and shop windows at this season of the year.

Almost all children gradually outgrow the idea of Santa Claus as they do other childish conceptions after they have served their purpose of training the emotional nature in the right direction. The transition is the more easily made if the child is gradually led to make and to give Christmas gifts to those he loves. Thus, as I have tried to show in a previous article, the mere material thought of Christmas as a time for a jolly lot of fun is gradually changed into the higher thought of a joyful festival, *through the child's own deeds*.

No mother need expect her child to understand the Christian Christmas by one celebration. His own experiences of the joy which arises from unselfish giving must be repeated many times before he can enter into the thought that God, in whose image he has been made, must have shown his love to mankind by some such manifestation as that which the celebration of Christmas commemorates.

V.

CHRISTMAS TIME. [2]

A memory which will always remain with me comes up as I approach the end of these chronicles. And although it did not arise from any one picture or song of the "Mother-Play-Book," it was caused by the Kindergarten study which had become part of our inmost life.

The long, dry season was over. Half a dozen rains had refreshed the land and caused it to blossom like a garden. It was hard to realize, midst the roses and lilies, tender green foliage and fragrant orange-blossoms, rippling streams and songs of mocking-birds, that Christmas was approaching; our northern minds had always associated the season with sleigh-bells and ice and snow, and yet it was amidst just such semitropical surroundings as these, that in the faraway Palestine was born the Babe, the celebration of whose returning birthday each year fills all Christendom with the spirit of self-sacrifice, love, and joy, and binds, as does no other festal day, a multitude of the human race into one common brotherhood.

Margaret and I decided that whatever else we did or did not do, during the remainder of our sojourn among the hills, the children should have a *real Christmas*. In order that we might make it an inner Christmas as well as an outer one, we began at the approach of Advent to show them how to make Christmas presents. It took no small amount of patience to pin down to definite work, which must be neatly and daintily done, the two little mortals who had lived almost as free from tasks as the lilies of the field. However, we both realized that the children must make a real effort to give genuinely to others something which they themselves had made, if they were to have the real joy which ought to come with the receiving of presents.

Far too often children accept Christmas presents as so many added, material possessions, not as expressions of love and service from others. We had both long ago learned that only he who gives can truly, spiritually receive, and that a gift without this comprehension of its inner meaning is no gift at all, but merely something gained which oftentimes awakens greed and selfishness.

Therefore, by dint of raising up visions of *how surprised* grossmutter would be when Christmas morning came and she received two presents made by four little hands she loved, by enacting in dramatic detail the astonishment which their father would show when he too should receive a present made by them, we succeeded in awakening in them sufficient ambition to attempt what was to both of them a disagreeable task. They had been willing enough to draw, cut, fold, mold, or paste anything which would serve as an illustration of a story in which they were interested, or which would revivify some pleasant personal experience; but to sit down and deliberately draw, or paint, or sew an object for somebody else, with the thought of making it pleasant to that person rather than to themselves, was a new idea.

First one and then the other of us would occasionally sew a flower upon a picture-frame when the little untrained fingers grew too tired; or we would adroitly exchange work, letting them bring in a pail of water from the spring while we put a strip or two in a gay gold-and-scarlet mat which was to be worked over into a Christmas present, thus bringing the end of the little task somewhat nearer. Occasionally, of course, a story would be told of some loving little child about whom even the fairies sang, because he or she worked hard to make Christmas gifts for loved ones. Sometimes Margaret would exclaim: "What do you suppose *the knights* would say if they should come riding up the road and see two dear children working away as hard as they could on their Christmas presents?"

The first two presents, for grossmutter and father, their two nearest relatives, were finished and daintily folded away in colored tissue paper, when Margaret had a whispered conversation with them and suggested that they should surprise me also with a Christmas present, and I, on a like occasion, proposed to them that they should surprise her with something at

Christmas time. Then followed days of whispered talk; of sudden hiding of work, or of gleeful shouting: "Go away! You mustn't come here now!"

Often there would be delighted covering up of the hands and lap at my approach, or at that of Margaret—scenes so common in the homes of Kindergarten-trained children, but so delightfully new to these little Arabs of the desert who had never, in all their short lives before, felt the dignity of individual, personal possessions which they could give away.

Our presents finished and mysteriously laid away, the next step was to lead to the thought of making presents for our next neighbor and his good wife, whose ranch was about half a mile away. This, of course, soon led on to the idea of having a Christmas present ready for *everybody*. There were only about five families in all on the foothills, but they constituted *everybody* to the children, whose world, dear souls, was bounded by the horizon which had its center in their own home; saving of course, that boundless world into which Margaret and I had introduced them through pictures and stories, where lived the mighty kings and queens, giants and genii, fairies and princesses, prophets and priests, and above all, *the knights*. This latter world of the imagination was such a grand world that it did not need presents.

Soon the two happy little hearts were overflowing with the true Christmas love; and the presents made by their own hands "for *everybody*" were laid out upon my bed and examined and exclaimed over. Each of these was again folded up in a bright piece of tissue paper and tied with a bit of narrow, daintily colored ribbon and labeled with the name of the person to whom it was to be given. All these long, busy days were so full of Christmas talks and songs and stories that they even yet bring back to me the feeling of having lived them in the midst of a great musical festival.

We had frequent occasion to cross the ranches belonging to our different neighbors, in our daily tramps over the foothills, and often met the men at their work or stopped to chat for a moment with the women in their doorways. At such times, Georgie would look up with a laughing face and sparkling eyes and say: "We've got somefin' for you for Christmas, but you mustn't know what it is."

And then, if the inquisitive neighbor would question, he would dance about and clap his hands, and shake his little head, saying: "No, no, no! Wait until Christmas comes, and then you shall see it; but we made it all ourselves."

"'Cept what *they* did to help us," the more conscientious Lena would add, as she pointed to Margaret or me.

We had found, as is not uncommon in sparsely settled districts, where there must necessarily be a struggle for a livelihood, that life among our neighbors had somewhat narrowed itself down to the material standpoint, and consequently, as always happens when this is the case, various frictions had occurred among them, leaving them not always in quite the neighborly attitude toward each other. But no one was able to resist the children's joyful over-flowing Christmas love.

In a short time it was settled among us all that the Christmas celebration should take place at Georgie's and Lena's home, and that all the neighbors should be present on Christmas Eve to see the lighting of the Christmas tree, which Margaret and I had decided was to be as gorgeous as our limited resources could make it.

In a little while first one and then another neighbor volunteered to help decorate the house; one offering to saw off and bring to us branches from an unusually beautiful pepper-tree; another volunteered his services in going to town for anything we might need; and a good housewife recalled the days when she was young and asked if we would like to have her make some ginger-bread boys and girls and animals to hang on the tree, and so on. Before long the children's spirit of enthusiasm and love for others had spread throughout our small foothill world, and everywhere we went we were greeted with smiles, significant nods, and occasional whispered conversations.

A few days before Christmas came, one of our foothill neighbors stopped us on the road to suggest that he should go down, on Christmas Eve, to the mesa below and bring up two little English children whose home had been saddened by the death of their father a few weeks before, and whose mother, being a stranger in California, had no friends to whom to go. Thus was the Christmas spirit overflowing the foothills and spreading on to the farther districts. Then some one else thought of a man and his wife and young baby who lived about six miles up the cañon, and they, too, were invited. All small grudges were forgotten and seemingly swallowed up in the coming festivities.

The contagion of love is as great as the contagion of disease or crime. Each time we finished a bit of trimming for the tree, which was yet to be selected, it had now to be taken down to be shown to Mrs. Middlin. As we passed the old wood-chopper he would make some light, laughing remark, and we occasionally stopped at his side to sing to him a new Christmas song which the children had just learned. He would at such times lay down his axe, and his wrinkled old face would become bright with the light of his far-away youth, as he looked down into the children's happy, eager eyes; and he usually sent us on our way with some such remark as, "Well, them children air great ones," or else it would be, "Children will be children. I used to be that way myself." The half-invalid woman, whom pain had made fretful and nervous, and who had been in the habit of declaring that all children were a nuisance and ought to be kept in their homes, could not resist Georgie's roguish shout, "I got somefin' for you Christmas! You must be sure to come up to see the Christmas tree." On the eventful day she actually did come with all the rest and brought with her some home-made candy, such as she used to make when she was a girl some forty odd years before.

This drawing together round the Christmas thought, each and every one making an effort to add something to the joy of the occasion, proved what every true lover of humanity believes, that deep down in each human heart is love and a desire to be loved, is joy in seeing others happy, and the greater joy of serving others.

In return for this unexpected volunteer addition to our plans for the children, Margaret and I contrived some trifle or joke for each man member of the community. To one it was a bundle of toothpicks done up in fancy tissue paper. To another it was a Mexican tamale. To a young fellow who worked on one of the ranches it was a candy sweetheart. For each of the women we made some trifle in the way of needle-book, iron-holder, or the like, as we wanted the children to have the pleasure of seeing their elders go up to the tree and receive gifts as well as themselves.

Three days before the Christmas Eve party the two children and their father, Margaret and I, went up the cañon to let the children select a small fir-tree for the Christmas tree. As we came triumphantly driving through a neighbor's ranch on our way home with the little tree in the back of the wagon, the children shouted out with great glee: "Come out! Come out! and see the tree! See the tree! Here it is! Here it is! The really, really Christmas tree!" And out came both gray-haired old neighbors, almost as much pleased as the children.

The tree was fastened between two boards, and then with great ceremony we marched in a procession into the little best room which their grandmother usually kept shut and unused, and placed it upon the table in the center of the room. Then began the exciting, and to the children most charming, work of decorating it with strings of popcorn and cranberries; and fancy chains made with the scarlet and blue, gilt and silver paper which loving hearts in the far-away Chicago had sent, helped make gorgeous our little tree. Some fancy pink and pale blue papers which had come from the drug store had been carefully saved for the occasion. Onto these we pasted narrow strips of the gold and silver paper, and "Chinese lanterns" were made, much to the delight of the children. Each afternoon we decorated the tree with the work which had been done in the morning, and then danced around it and sang songs to it, and told it stories about other little Christmas trees which had made other little children happy.

One day Georgie improvised a song, and like the poet of old, danced in rhythm to the melody which he himself created to the tune of "Heigh-ho, the way we go." The words were as follows:

> "Miss Margaret and I
> We wish we could fly,
> Heigh-ho, heigh-ho, under the Christmas tree.
> We sing now for joy,
> The girl and the boy,
> Heigh-ho, heigh-ho, under the Christmas tree."

He had undoubtedly caught the rhythm, and perhaps the refrain, from some verses which Margaret had written about our mountain home, and whose refrain was "Heigh-ho, heigh-ho, under the greenwood-tree." But I was much pleased to see his original application of the idea, and his feeling of the fitness of the festival occasion for improvised verse. It seemed to bubble out of the fullness of his joy just as many a refrain and love song of old was born on festival occasions; so close is the child akin to the child race.

Some time before this Margaret had brought from her mysterious trunk a small and very beautiful copy of the Mother and Child which forms the center of Correggio's great picture, "The Holy Night," and Lena had sewed a round picture frame, designed by Margaret, with a gold star on the upper corner and a modest little violet on the lower, symbolic, it seemed to me, of the exaltation and humility which that picture so marvelously portrays. It was to be a joint gift from Margaret and Lena to the dear old grossmutter. The children had both sat and studied the two beautiful faces, so luminous with light; and Margaret had explained to them that the light came from the dear baby's face and shone into that of the mother because this dear little Christ Child had just come from God and the mother knew it.

"That is what makes her so happy," said Georgie, and Margaret answered, "Yes, that is what makes every good mother happy when she looks into her baby's face," and Georgie had accepted this somewhat broad interpretation of the picture with one of his significant nods. So far as we could ascertain, the children had as yet no training whatever in biblical lore, and our plan had been that we would speak only in general terms of the Bible story of Christmas until after they had experienced the love and joy of service and giving. Then we would tell them why not only their little world, but the whole great big world of Christendom celebrated the day with such joy. But suddenly one evening, as we were returning from our hilltop scramble, Lena said, "Grossmutter knows all about the dear little Christ Child, and she says the angels knew that He was coming."

"Let's sit down here by this rock," said Georgie, "and then you can tell us all about it." He had implicit faith that Margaret could tell him all about anything he wished to know, so he never hesitated to make the demand.

We sat down on the ground, with sky above us radiant and glowing in sunset's splendor, and Margaret told, as I had never heard it told before, of the watching of the shepherds and of the coming of the angels, and when she came to the part, "and as the shepherds raised their bodies up from the ground and listened and listened, the far-away music came nearer and nearer, and then they saw that the music was the singing of countless numbers of beautiful angels, and that the bright light which had slowly spread over the whole heavens came from the beauty of their faces; the whole sky seemed full of them, and they were all singing joyfully the first Christmas song that was ever heard on earth," Georgie rose from his half-reclining position and coming close to Margaret placed his hands upon her shoulder and said, eagerly: "Sing it! Sing it! Sing it just as the angels sang it!"

She afterwards told me that she would have given five years of her life to have had Patti's voice for just that one hour. She quietly replied: "I cannot sing it, Georgie, as the angels sang it. No one on earth can sing it as the angels sang it on the first glad Christmas night, but we can know what they meant to tell the shepherds."

He turned his face away from her with a look of disappointment, and his eyes wandered far over the hills to the glowing sky, then quickly turning toward us, he said, "Maybe the Christmas angels will come now. Let us listen and see if we can hear them."

Then we listened silently until the light began to fade out of the evening sky, and Margaret said: "I can tell you what the words were which the angels sang, and perhaps we can feel their song down in our hearts."

And then slowly and reverently she repeated the old, yet ever new, message to mankind: "Glory to God in the highest. Peace on earth, good will to men!" And gently added, by way of explanation, that good will to men meant that we were all brothers and sisters in God's sight, and that this was one of the great things which the dear Christ Child came to teach us. "And this," she added, "is why we celebrate His birthday by making gifts for 'everybody.'" Both children nodded assent in a matter-of-course way. They, dear little hearts, did not yet know the schisms and discords that sometimes separate brothers and sisters, and to them it was a matter of course, that men should accept the angelic message.

As we walked home, Georgie skipping and dancing along in front, sang, "I love everybody! I love everybody! I am so happy! I am so happy! I love everybody!"

"So do I, Georgie," said Margaret, earnestly; and I think for the time being, at least, all of us felt the true Christmas spirit. That motto from Froebel's "Mother-Play-Songs" came into my mind with a new meaning:

"Would'st thou unite the child for aye with thee, Then let him with the Highest One thy union see By every noble thought thy heart is fired, The young child's soul will surely be inspired. And thou can'st no better gift bestow, Than union with the Eternal One to know."

We quickened our steps as we neared home, and all four of us sang softly—

"In anther land and clime,
Long ago and far away."

The morning of Christmas Eve brought to us our friend, Mrs. Brown, who had a Kindergarten in a neighboring town. Her contribution to the festive occasion was a box of fifty small wax candles, and we proceeded at once to add the final touches for the evening entertainment. A frieze had already been made around the walls of the room with branches of the pepper-tree, whose feathery green leaves and coral-colored branches of berries made a beautiful decoration. Large bunches of the dark green eucalyptus had been sawed off and so arranged that they made frames of the green around the two windows whose white curtains the good grossmutter had washed and ironed the day before. In the center of the room was the Christmas tree on which hung the treasures worked by little hands. The red, green, and yellow candles were fastened in the safer parts of the horizontal branches; others were placed around the table on candlesticks made of ripe oranges; and a row of these golden candlesticks was also placed upon the edge of a wooden shelf which had held the grossmutter's German Bible. The ugly woolen cover of the shelf was entirely concealed by soft green ferns. A pound or two of candy had been purchased by the father, and this the dear old grandmother, with trembling but eager hands, showed us how to tie up with strings of worsted and fasten to the tree, "just as they used to do in the faterland," she explained to the children. Her joy over the whole affair was, if anything, greater than that of the little ones. She insisted that Mrs. Brown, Margaret, and I should be her guests at the noonday dinner; and her appreciation of our work was shown by the killing of the fatted goose, and by boiling and baking and stewing, in true German fashion, about three times the quantity of food which we could possibly consume. During the getting ready of this dinner she bustled in and out of the little parlor, sometimes throwing her arms around the children and exclaiming, "Oh, Chorgie! Chorgie! Dis is just like a Christmas in the old country! Just tink of it! Just tink of it! Mine kinder are to have a German Christmas! A real German Christmas!" Then, as if fearing that her emotions should be taken for weakness, she buffeted them severely with her hand and pushed them to one side with the words, "Keep out of de way! Don't talk so much! You are little nuisances anyhow!" but with so much love in the tone that the rebuking words were unheeded. Again, she would come into the room and stand with her hands resting upon her hips and gaze silently, with unspeakable satisfaction, at the busy scene before her.

In making our plans for the evening, Margaret turned and said in a tone of quiet respect: "Frau Zorn, we will, of course, expect you to stand with the children and us, and receive the guests. It is your party, you know, as well as the children's. We are merely helping to get it ready."

"Oh, mein dear! Mein dear!" exclaimed the old lady, evidently much pleased with the unexpected prominence which was to be given to her. Without further words she bustled out of the room, and in about a half-hour called to Margaret and me to come up into the little attic above. There we found her on her knees before an old horsehair trunk out of which she had taken a black and gray striped silk gown of the fashion of about twenty years before; also a soft white silk neck handkerchief. In an embarrassed tone, looking half-ashamed, half-proud, she said: "I had laid dem away for my burying clothes, but I can wear dem to-night, if you tink it best."

"Certainly," exclaimed Margaret; "that dress is just the thing, and the pretty white handkerchief will make you look young again. I am so glad you have them. I will come in time to arrange your hair and I have a wee bit of a lace handkerchief which I know how to fix into a cap, just such as my own grandmother used to wear, and you will be the handsomest part of the whole Christmas entertainment." Then she added in great glee: "Don't let the children see the dress until after you put it on. It will be such a lovely surprise for them."

The old woman's face showed how keen this simple pleasure was to her as she softly patted the dress, straightening here and there a bit of its old-fashioned trimming, and then laid it gently into the trunk until the appointed hour should come.

The morning work was at last ended, including our most conscientious endeavors to do justice to the elaborate dinner. We locked the door of the little parlor fearing that the temptation to meddle with the wax candles might be too great to be resisted. Handing the key to Frau Zorn and giving our "Christmas kiss" to each of the children, somewhat tired we went back to our little cabin to rest until the evening. We had promised to come early so as to be there before the first guests should arrive, and just before starting out on our return Margaret quietly gathered a basketful of beautiful La France roses which were blossoming in bewildering profusion near our doorstep.

"What are you going to do with those?" I asked. "Make every man and woman who comes to-night feel that he or she is in true festival attire," she answered, smiling. And sure enough as each guest came in, Lena, by Margaret's instructions, asked the privilege of pinning a Christmas rose upon the man's coat and the woman's dress. The smile with which the unaccustomed decoration was accepted showed the wisdom of Margaret's plan. An added festivity came over the scene, and each individual felt himself or herself duly decorated for the occasion.

When the man from the cañon beyond arrived with his wife and the little three-months-old baby, Georgie's face was a study worthy of Raphael's brush; confusion, surprise, pleasure, joy were all commingled, as looking up to Margaret, he exclaimed, "Why, Miss Marg't! We are going to have a *real, truly baby* at our Christmas time!" Then, lowering his voice, "Perhaps it will be like the Christ baby and we can see the light shining from it just as the shepherds saw it."

The guests had been invited into the little dining-room which was the usual sitting-room of the family, and the parlor was kept closed. At a signal from Margaret, the father of the two children walked forward, and throwing the door open, invited the guests to walk in. It was lighted entirely by the wax candles, which gave that peculiar mellow light suggestive of silent and reverent feeling that the Roman Catholic Church has been wise enough to seize upon and make use of.

The hilarious laughter and somewhat awkward jokes which had been going on ceased for the time being. When all were seated on the benches and the improvised seats which had been brought in, Margaret and the children sang two or three Christmas songs. Then, as a surprise to the rest of us, they clustered around the dear old grossmutter and the four, bowing, joined in a German hymn of praise and thanksgiving. This was intended as a surprise to the father and to me, and was indeed a surprise to all of us, as none of the neighbors had ever heard the dear old woman sing.

Then came the distribution of presents, and the laughter and jokes and fun such as happy hearts improvise and enjoy. One neighbor had brought an old-fashioned hat-box labeled "For Lena and Georgie." When opened, out sprang two frisky little kittens that, in a frightened fashion, scampered away under the protecting skirts of some of the women, but were soon captured and caressed with delight by the little owners. The same thoughtful neighbor had brought two little chickens for the little English children from the mesa below. They were less lively, but were tenderly cared for by the children.

Finally, when all the presents had been distributed, including part of the fruit and candy, two of the men laughingly disappeared from the room, and on their return, brought between them a huge California pumpkin, which measured five and one-half feet around its circumference. This had previously been prepared into what they called a "Christmas box," the top had been cut smoothly off, and into it had been fastened the handle of a bucket. The lower part had been hollowed out, washed, and dried; the pumpkin seemed almost large enough to have served as a carriage for Cinderella. It was placed at Margaret's feet, and the top lifted off amidst shouts of laughter and the clapping of hands. Each guest present had stored away in it some loving little gift, of no value whatever so far as the world considers value, but rich indeed to one who prizes a gift according to the loving thought which it shows. One woman had pasted upon several sheets of writing paper some rare ferns and mosses which she had brought from the mountains of New Mexico years before, and had sewed them together in the form of a book. Another had embroidered Margaret's initials upon a Chinese silk scarf, which had been one of her treasures in the days of greater prosperity. Another had rounded off and polished a pin-cushion of Yoca wood, sawed from a stalk in the higher mountain districts. The fourth had made her a shell-box, of shells gathered on some past trip to the Cataline Islands. A fifth had heard her express a desire to make a collection of the different kinds of wood which grew in the neighborhood and had brought carefully sawed and neatly polished specimens of a half-dozen varieties, and so on; each showing that her taste had been remembered, some wish expressed at an odd moment had been recalled, or some pleasant surprise anticipated.

Margaret's eyes filled with tears as one by one she unfolded these gifts of love; then, realizing that such a time as the present needed more joy than anything else, she laughingly brushed away the unshed tears and proposed that they should all enter into some games together. This was heartily agreed to by the others, and the evening ended in almost a romp. Hands were shaken, good bys were said, the last joke uttered, and wagon and gig and buggy drove away.

Margaret, Mrs. Brown, and I remained to help put the children to bed and somewhat straighten up the little house. Then bidding the happy-faced old woman "Good by," we started out, alone, for a quiet walk across the hill, under the Christmas stars. As we prepared for bed Margaret exclaimed, "What a happy, happy day we have had!" I looked into her radiant face, and said, softly, to myself: "*Blessed be motherhood, even if it must be the motheringofotherwomen'schildr   en*!"

VI.

A CHRISTMAS CAROL.

STAVE ONE.

MARLEY'S GHOST.

[We hardly know of anything better to recommend than the following exquisite masterpiece of Dickens, for hearts that have grown dull to the real joy of Christmas tide.]

Marley was dead, to begin with. There is no doubt whatever about that. The register of his burial was signed by the clergyman, the clerk, the undertaker, and the chief mourner. Scrooge signed it. And Scrooge's name was good upon 'Change for anything he chose to put his hand to.

Old Marley was as dead as a door-nail.

Mind! I don't mean to say that I know, of my own knowledge, what there is particularly dead about a door-nail. I might have been inclined, myself, to regard a coffin-nail as the deadest piece of ironmongery in the trade. But the wisdom of our ancestors is in the simile; and my unhallowed hands shall not disturb it, or the country's done for. You will therefore permit me to repeat, emphatically, that Marley was as dead as a door-nail.

Scrooge knew he was dead? Of course he did. How could it be otherwise? Scrooge and he were partners for I don't know how many years. Scrooge was his sole executor, his sole administrator, his sole assign, his sole residuary legatee, his sole friend, and sole mourner. And even Scrooge was not so dreadfully cut up by the sad event but that he was an excellent man of business on the very day of the funeral, and solemnized it with an undoubted bargain.

The mention of Marley's funeral brings me back to the point I started from. There is no doubt that Marley was dead. This must be distinctly understood, or nothing wonderful can come of the story I am going to relate. If we were not perfectly convinced that Hamlet's father died before the play began, there would be nothing more remarkable in his taking a stroll at night, in an easterly wind, upon his own ramparts, than there would be in any other middle-aged gentleman rashly turning out after dark in a breezy spot—say Saint Paul's churchyard, for instance—literally to astonish his son's weak mind.

Scrooge never painted out old Marley's name. There it stood, years afterwards, above the warehouse door: Scrooge and Marley. The firm was known as Scrooge and Marley. Sometimes people new to the business called Scrooge, Scrooge, and sometimes Marley, but he answered to both names. It was all the same to him.

Oh, but he was a tight-fisted hand at the grindstone, Scrooge! a squeezing, wrenching, grasping, scraping, clutching, covetous, old sinner! Hard and sharp as flint, from which no steel had ever struck out generous fire; secret, and self-contained, and solitary as an oyster. The cold within him froze his old features, nipped his pointed nose, shriveled his cheek, stiffened his gait; made his eyes red, his thin lips blue; and spoke out shrewdly in his grating voice. A frosty rime was on his head, and on his eyebrows, and his wiry chin. He carried his own low temperature always about with him; he iced his office in the dog-days, and didn't thaw it one degree at Christmas.

External heat and cold had little influence on Scrooge. No warmth could warm, no wintry weather chill him. No wind that blew was bitterer than he, no falling snow was more intent upon its purpose, no pelting rain less open to entreaty. Foul weather didn't know where to have him. The heaviest rain, and snow, and hail, and sleet, could boast of the advantage over him in only one respect—they often "came down" handsomely, and Scrooge never did.

Nobody ever stopped him in the street to say, with gladsome looks, "My dear Scrooge, how are you? When will you come to see me?" No beggars implored him to bestow a trifle, no children asked him what it was o'clock, no man or woman ever once in all his life inquired the way to such and such a place, of Scrooge. Even the blind men's dogs appeared to know him; and when they saw him coming on, would tug their owners into doorways and up courts; and then would wag their tails as though they said, "No eye at all is better than an evil eye, dark master!"

But what did Scrooge care! It was the very thing he liked. To edge his way along the crowded paths of life, warning all human sympathy to keep its distance, was what the knowing ones call "nuts" to Scrooge.

Once upon a time—of all the good days in the year, on Christmas Eve—old Scrooge sat busy in his counting-house. It was cold, bleak, biting weather, foggy withal, and he could hear the people in the court outside go wheezing up and down, beating their hands upon their breasts, and stamping their feet upon the pavement stones to warm them. The city clocks had only just gone three, but it was quite dark already—it had not been light all day—and candles were flaring in the windows of the neighboring offices, like ruddy smears upon the palpable brown air. The fog came pouring in at every chink and key-hole, and was so dense without, that although the court was of the narrowest, the houses opposite were mere phantoms. To see the dingy cloud come drooping down, obscuring everything, one might have thought that nature lived hard by, and was brewing on a large scale.

The door of Scrooge's counting-house was open that he might keep his eye upon his clerk, who in a dismal little cell beyond, a sort of tank, was copying letters. Scrooge had a very small fire, but the clerk's fire was so very much smaller that it looked like one coal. But he couldn't replenish it, for Scrooge kept the coal-box in his own room; and so surely as the clerk came in with the shovel, the master predicted that it would be necessary for them to part. Wherefore the clerk put on his white comforter, and tried to warm himself at the candle; in which effort, not being a man of a strong imagination, he failed.

"A merry Christmas, uncle! God save you!" cried a cheerful voice. It was the voice of Scrooge's nephew, who came upon him so quickly that this was the first intimation he had of his approach.

"Bah!" said Scrooge, "Humbug!"

He had so heated himself with rapid walking in the fog and frost, this nephew of Scrooge's, that he was all in a glow; his face was ruddy and handsome; his eyes sparkled, and his breath smoked again.

"Christmas a humbug, uncle!" said Scrooge's nephew. "You don't mean that, I am sure."

"I do," said Scrooge. "Merry Christmas! What right have you to be merry? What reason have you to be merry? You're poor enough."

"Come, then," returned the nephew, gayly. "What right have you to be dismal? What reason have you to be morose? You're rich enough."

Scrooge having no better answer ready on the spur of the moment, said "Bah!" again; and followed it up with "Humbug!"

"Don't be cross, uncle!" said the nephew.

"What else can I be," returned the uncle, "when I live in such a world of fools as this? Merry Christmas! Out upon merry Christmas! What's Christmas time to you but a time for paying bills without money; a time for finding yourself a year older, but not an hour richer; a time for balancing your books and having every item in 'em through a round dozen of months presented dead against you? If I could work my will," said Scrooge, indignantly, "every idiot who goes about with 'Merry Christmas' on his lips, should be boiled with his own pudding, and buried with a stake of holly through his heart. He should!"

"Uncle!" pleaded the nephew.

"Nephew!" returned the uncle, sternly, "keep Christmas in your own way, and let me keep it in mine."

"Keep it," repeated Scrooge's nephew, "but you don't keep it."

"Let me leave it alone, then," said Scrooge. "Much good may it do you! Much good it has ever done you!"

"There are many things from which I might have derived good, by which I have not profited, I dare say," returned the nephew, "Christmas among the rest. But I am sure I have always thought of Christmas time, when it has come round—apart from the veneration due to its sacred name and origin, if anything belonging to it can be apart from that—as a good time; a kind, forgiving, charitable, pleasant time; the only time I know of, in the long calendar of the year, when men and women seem by one consent to open their shut-up hearts freely, and to think of people below them as if they really were fellow-passengers to the grave, and not another race of creatures bound on other journeys. And therefore, uncle, though it has never put a scrap of gold or silver in my pocket, I believe that it *has* done me good, and *will* do me good; and I say, God bless it!"

The clerk in the tank involuntarily applauded. Becoming immediately sensible of the impropriety, he poked the fire, and extinguished the last frail spark forever.

"Let me hear another sound from *you*," said Scrooge, "and you'll keep your Christmas by losing your situation! You're quite a powerful speaker, sir," he added, turning to his nephew. "I wonder you don't go into Parliament."

"Don't be angry, uncle. Come dine with us to-morrow."

Scrooge said that he would see him—yes, indeed he did. He went the whole length of the expression, and said that he would see him in that extremity first.

"But why?" cried Scrooge's nephew. "Why?"

"Why did you get married?" said Scrooge.

"Because I fell in love."

"Because you fell in love!" growled Scrooge, as if that were the only one thing in the world more ridiculous than a merry Christmas. "Good afternoon!"

"Nay, uncle, but you never came to see me before that happened. Why give it as a reason for not coming now?"

"Good afternoon," said Scrooge.

"I want nothing from you; I ask nothing of you; why cannot we be friends?"

"Good afternoon," said Scrooge.

"I am sorry, with all my heart, to find you so resolute. We have never had any quarrel, to which I have been a party. But I have made the trial in homage to Christmas, and I'll keep my Christmas humor to the last. So, a merry Christmas, uncle!"

"Good afternoon!" said Scrooge.

"And a happy New Year!"

His nephew left the room without an angry word, notwithstanding. He stopped at the outer door to bestow the greetings of the season on the clerk, who, cold as he was, was warmer than Scrooge; for he returned them cordially.

"There's another fellow," muttered Scrooge, who overheard him: "my clerk, with fifteen shillings a week, and a wife and family, talking about a merry Christmas. I'll retire to Bedlam."

This lunatic, in letting Scrooge's nephew out, had let two other people in. They were portly gentlemen, pleasant to behold, and now stood, with their hats off, in Scrooge's office. They had books and papers in their hands, and bowed to him.

"Scrooge and Marley's, I believe," said one of the gentlemen, referring to his list. "Have I the pleasure of addressing Mr. Scrooge, or Mr. Marley?"

"Mr. Marley has been dead these seven years," Scrooge replied. "He died seven years ago, this very night."

"We have no doubt his liberality is well represented by his surviving partner," said the gentleman, presenting his credentials.

It certainly was; for they had been two kindred spirits. At the ominous word "liberality," Scrooge frowned, and shook his head, and handed the credentials back.

"At this festive season of the year, Mr. Scrooge," said the gentleman, taking up a pen, "it is more than usually desirable that we should make some provision for the poor and destitute, who suffer greatly at the present time. Many thousands are in want of common necessaries; hundreds of thousands are in want of common comforts, sir."

"Are there no prisons?" asked Scrooge.

"Plenty of prisons," said the gentleman, laying down the pen again.

"And the Union workhouses?" demanded Scrooge. "Are they still in operation?"

"They are. Still," returned the gentleman, "I wish I could say they were not."

"The Treadmill and the Poor Law are in full vigor, then?" said Scrooge.

"Both very busy, sir."

"Oh! I was afraid, from what you said at first, that something had occurred to stop them in their useful course," said Scrooge. "I'm very glad to hear it."

"Under the impression that they scarcely furnish Christian cheer of mind or body to the multitude," returned the gentleman, "a few of us are endeavoring to raise a fund to buy the poor some meat and drink, and means of warmth. We choose this time, because it is a time, of all others, when want is keenly felt, and abundance rejoices. What shall I put you down for?"

"Nothing!" Scrooge replied.

"You wish to be anonymous?"

"I wish to be left alone," said Scrooge. "Since you ask me what I wish, gentlemen, that is my answer. I don't make merry myself at Christmas, and I can't afford to make idle people merry. I help to support the establishments I have mentioned—they cost enough; and those who are badly off must go there."

"Many can't go there, and many would rather die."

"If they would rather die," said Scrooge, "they had better do it, and decrease the surplus population. Besides—excuse me—I don't know that."

"But you might know it," observed the gentleman.

"It's not my business," Scrooge returned. "It's enough for a man to understand his own business, and not to interfere with other people's. Mine occupies me constantly. Good afternoon, gentlemen!"

Seeing clearly that it would be useless to pursue their point, the gentlemen withdrew. Scrooge resumed his labors with an improved opinion of himself, and in a more facetious temper than was usual with him.

Meanwhile the fog and darkness thickened so that people ran about with flaring links, proffering their services to go before horses in carriages, and conduct them on their way. The ancient tower of a church, whose gruff old bell was always peeping slily down at Scrooge out of a gothic window in the wall, became invisible, and struck the hours and quarters in the clouds, with tremulous vibrations afterwards as if its teeth were chattering in its frozen head up there. The cold became intense. In the main street, at the corner of the court, some laborers were repairing the gas-pipes, and had lighted a great fire in a brazier, round which a party of ragged men and boys were gathered, warming their hands and winking their eyes before the blaze in rapture. The water-plug being left in solitude, its overflowings sullenly congealed, and turned to misanthropic ice. The brightness of the shops where holly sprigs and berries crackled in the lamp heat of the windows made pale faces ruddy as they passed. Poulterers' and grocers' trades became a splendid joke: a glorious pageant, with which it was next to impossible to believe that such dull principles as bargain and sale had anything to do. The Lord Mayor, in the stronghold of the mighty Mansion House, gave orders to his fifty cooks and butlers to keep Christmas as a Lord Mayor's household should; and even the little tailor, whom he had fined five shillings on the previous Monday for being drunk and bloodthirsty in the streets, stirred up to-morrow's pudding in his garret, while his lean wife and the baby sallied out to buy the beef.

Foggier yet, and colder! Piercing, searching, biting cold. If the good Saint Dunstan had but nipped the evil spirit's nose with a touch of such weather as that, instead of using his familiar weapons, then indeed he would have roared to lusty purpose. The owner of one scant young nose, gnawed and mumbled by the hungry cold as bones are gnawed by dogs, stooped down at Scrooge's keyhole to regale him with a Christmas carol; but at the first sound of

"God bless you, merry gentleman!
May nothing you dismay!"

Scrooge seized the ruler with such energy of action that the singer fled in terror, leaving the keyhole to the fog and even more congenial frost.

At length the hour of shutting up the counting-house arrived. With an ill will Scrooge dismounted from his stool, and tacitly admitted the fact to the expectant clerk in the tank, who instantly snuffed his candle out, and put on his hat.

"You'll want all day to-morrow, I suppose?" said Scrooge.

"If quite convenient, sir."

"It's not convenient," said Scrooge, "and it's not fair. If I was to stop half-a-crown for it, you'd think yourself ill used, I'll be bound?"

The clerk smiled faintly.

"And yet," said Scrooge, "you don't think me ill used when I pay a day's wages for no work."

The clerk observed that it was only once a year.

"A poor excuse for picking a man's pocket every twenty-fifth of December!" said Scrooge, buttoning his greatcoat to the chin. "But I suppose you must have the whole day. Be here all the earlier next morning."

The clerk promised that he would; and Scrooge walked out with a growl. The office was closed in a twinkling, and the clerk, with the long ends of his white comforter dangling below his waist (for he boasted no greatcoat), went down a slide on Cornhill, at the end of a lane of boys, twenty times, in honor of its being Christmas Eve, and then ran home to Camden Town as hard as he could pelt, to play at blindman's-buff.

Scrooge took his melancholy dinner in his usual melancholy tavern; and having read all the newspapers, and beguiled the rest of the evening with his banker's-book, went home to bed. He lived in chambers which had once belonged to his deceased partner. They were a gloomy suite of rooms, in a lowering pile of building up a yard, where it had so little business to be that one could scarcely help fancying it must have run there when it was a young house, playing at hide-and-seek with other houses, and forgotten the way out again. It was old enough now, and dreary enough, for nobody lived in it but Scrooge, the other rooms being all let out as offices. The yard was so dark that even Scrooge, who knew its every stone, was fain to grope with his hands. The fog and frost so hung about the black old gateway of the house that it seemed as if the Genius of the Weather sat in mournful meditation on the threshold.

Now, it is a fact that there was nothing at all particular about the knocker on the door, except that it was very large. It is also a fact that Scrooge had seen it, night and morning, during his whole residence in that place; also that Scrooge had as little of what is called fancy about him as any man in the city of London, even including—which is a bold word—the corporation, aldermen, and livery. Let it also be borne in mind that Scrooge had not bestowed one thought on Marley since his last mention of his seven-years' dead partner that afternoon. And then let any man explain to me, if he can, how it happened that Scrooge, having his key in the lock of the door, saw in the knocker, without its undergoing any intermediate process of change— not a knocker, but Marley's face.

Marley's face. It was not in impenetrable shadow as the other objects in the yard were, but had a dismal light about it, like a bad lobster in a dark cellar. It was not angry or ferocious, but looked at Scrooge as Marley used to look, with ghostly spectacles turned up on its ghostly forehead. The hair was curiously stirred, as if by breath or hot air; and though the eyes were wide open, they were perfectly motionless. That, and its livid color, made it horrible; but its horror seemed to be in spite of the face and beyond its control, rather than a part of its own expression.

As Scrooge looked fixedly at this phenomenon, it was a knocker again.

To say that he was not startled, or that his blood was not conscious of a terrible sensation to which it had been a stranger from infancy, would be untrue. But he put his hand upon the key he had relinquished, turned it sturdily, walked in, and lighted his candle.

He *did* pause, with a moment's irresolution, before he shut the door; and he *did* look cautiously behind at first, as if he half-expected to be terrified with the sight of Marley's pigtail sticking out into the hall. But there was nothing on the back of the door, except the screws and nuts that held the knocker on, so he said, "Pooh, pooh!" and closed it with a bang.

The sound resounded through the house like thunder. Every room above, and every cask in the wine-merchant's cellars below, appeared to have a separate peal of echoes of its own. Scrooge was not a man to be frightened by echoes. He fastened the door and walked across the hall, and up the stairs, slowly too, trimming his candle as he went.

You may talk vaguely about driving a coach-and-six up a good old flight of stairs, or through a bad young act of Parliament; but I mean to say you might have got a hearse up that stair-case, and taken it broadwise, with the splinter-bar towards the wall and the door towards the balustrades, and done it easy. There was plenty of width for that, and room to spare; which is perhaps the reason why Scrooge thought he saw a locomotive hearse going on before him in the gloom. Half-a-dozen gas-lamps out of the street wouldn't have lighted the entry too well, so you may suppose that it was pretty dark with Scrooge's dip.

Up Scrooge went, not caring a button for that. Darkness is cheap, and Scrooge liked it. But before he shut his heavy door, he walked through his rooms to see that all was right. He had just enough recollection of the face to desire to do that.

Sitting-room, bedroom, lumber-room. All as they should be. Nobody under the table; nobody under the sofa; a small fire in the grate; spoon and basin ready; and the little sauce-pan of gruel (Scrooge had a cold in his head) upon the hob. Nobody under the bed; nobody in the closet; nobody in his dressing-gown, which was hanging up in a suspicious attitude against the wall. Lumber-room as usual. Old fire-guard, old shoes, two fish-baskets, washing-stand on three legs, and a poker.

Quite satisfied, he closed his door, and locked himself in; double-locked himself in, which was not his custom. Thus secured against surprise, he took off his cravat; put on his dressing-gown and slippers, and his night-cap, and sat down before the fire to take his gruel.

It was a very low fire indeed; nothing on such a bitter night. He was obliged to sit close to it, and brood over it before he could extract the least sensation of warmth from such a handful of fuel. The fireplace was an old one, built by some Dutch merchant long ago, and paved all round with quaint Dutch tiles, designed to illustrate the Scriptures. There were Cains and Abels,

Pharaoh's daughters, Queens of Sheba, Angelic messengers descending through the air on clouds like feather-beds, Abrahams, Belshazzars, Apostles putting off to sea in butter-boats, hundreds of figures to attract his thoughts; and yet that face of Marley, seven years dead, came like the ancient Prophet's rod, and swallowed up the whole. If each smooth tile had been a blank at first, with power to shape some picture on its surface from the disjointed fragments of his thoughts, there would have been a copy of old Marley's head on every one.

"Humbug!" said Scrooge, and walked across the room.

After several turns, he sat down again. As he threw his head back in the chair, his glance happened to rest upon a bell, a disused bell that hung in the room, and communicated, for some purpose now forgotten, with a chamber in the highest story of the building. It was with great astonishment, and with a strange, inexplicable dread, that as he looked, he saw this bell begin to swing. It swung so softly in the outset that it scarcely made a sound, but soon it rang out loudly, and so did every bell in the house.

This might have lasted half a minute, or a minute, but it seemed an hour. The bells ceased as they had begun, together. They were succeeded by a clanking noise, deep down below, as if some person were dragging a heavy chain over the casks in the wine merchant's cellar. Scrooge then remembered to have heard that ghosts in haunted houses were described as dragging chains.

The cellar door flew open with a booming sound, and then he heard the noise much louder on the floors below; then coming up the stairs; then coming straight towards his door.

"It's humbug, still!" said Scrooge. "I won't believe it."

His color changed though, when, without a pause, it came on through the heavy door, and passed into the room before his eyes. Upon its coming in the dying flame leaped up, as though it cried, "I know him; Marley's Ghost!" and fell again.

The same face; the very same. Marley in his pigtail, usual waistcoat, tights, and boots; the tassels on the latter bristling, like his pigtail, and his coat-skirts, and the hair upon his head. The chain he drew was clasped about his middle. It was long, and wound about him like a tail; and it was made (for Scrooge observed it closely) of cash-boxes, keys, padlocks, ledgers, deeds, and heavy purses wrought in steel. His body was transparent: so that Scrooge, observing him, and looking through his waistcoat, could see the two buttons on his coat behind.

Scrooge had often heard it said that Marley had no bowels, but he had never believed it until now.

No, nor did he believe it even now. Though he looked the phantom through and through, and saw it standing before him, though he felt the chilling influence of his death-cold eyes, and marked the very texture of the folded 'kerchief bound about its head and chin, which wrapper he had not observed before, he was still incredulous, and fought against his senses.

"How now!" said Scrooge, caustic and cold as ever. "What do you want with me?"

"Much!"—Marley's voice, no doubt about it.

"Who are you?"

"Ask me who I *was*."

"Who *were* you, then?" said Scrooge, raising his voice. "You're particular, for a shade." He was going to say "*to* a shade," but substituted this, as more appropriate.

"In life I was your partner, Jacob Marley."

"Can you—can you sit down?" asked Scrooge, looking doubtfully at him.

"I can."

"Do it, then."

Scrooge asked the question because he didn't know whether a ghost so transparent might find himself in a condition to take a chair; and felt that in the event of its being impossible, it might involve the necessity of an embarrassing explanation. But the Ghost sat down on the opposite side of the fireplace, as if he were quite used to it.

"You don't believe in me," observed the Ghost.

"I don't," said Scrooge.

"What evidence would you have of my reality beyond that of your senses?"

"I don't know," said Scrooge.

"Why do you doubt your senses?"

"Because," said Scrooge, "a little thing affects them. A slight disorder of the stomach makes them cheats. You may be an undigested bit of beef, a blot of mustard, a crumb of cheese, a fragment of an underdone potato. There's more of gravy than of grave about you, whatever you are."

Scrooge was not much in the habit of cracking jokes, nor did he feel, in his heart, by any means waggish then. The truth is, that he tried to be smart, as a means of distracting his own attention and keeping down his terror; for the Specter's voice disturbed the very marrow in his bones.

To sit staring at those fixed, glazed eyes in silence for a moment would play, Scrooge felt, the very deuce with him. There was something very awful, too, in the Specter's being provided with an infernal atmosphere of its own. Scrooge could not feel it himself, but this was clearly the case; for though the Ghost sat perfectly motionless, its hair, and skirts, and tassels were still agitated as by the hot vapor from an oven.

"You see this toothpick?" said Scrooge, returning quickly to the charge, for the reason just assigned, and wishing, though it were only for a second, to divert the vision's stony gaze from himself.

"I do," replied the Ghost.

"You are not looking at it," said Scrooge.

"But I see it," said the Ghost, "notwithstanding."

"Well," returned Scrooge, "I have but to swallow this, and be for the rest of my days persecuted by a legion of goblins, all of my own creation. Humbug, I tell you! Humbug!"

At this the spirit raised a frightful cry, and shook its chain with such a dismal and appalling noise that Scrooge held on tight to his chair to save himself from falling in a swoon. But how much greater was his horror when the phantom taking off the bandage round its head, as if it were too warm to wear indoors, its lower jaw dropped down upon its breast!

Scrooge fell upon his knees, and clasped his hands before his face.

"Mercy!" he said. "Dreadful apparition, why do you trouble me?"

"Man of the worldly mind," replied the Ghost, "do you believe in me or not?"

"I do," said Scrooge. "I must. But why do spirits walk the earth, and why do they come to me?"

"It is required of every man," the Ghost returned, "that the spirit within him should walk abroad among his fellowmen, and travel far and wide; and if that spirit goes not forth in life, it is condemned to do so after death. It is doomed to wander through the world—oh, woe is me!—and witness what it cannot share, but might have shared on earth, and turned to happiness!"

Again the Specter raised a cry and shook its chain and wrung its shadowy hands.

"You are fettered," said Scrooge, trembling. "Tell me why?"

"I wear the chain I forged in life," replied the Ghost. "I made it link by link, and yard by yard; I girded it on of my own free will, and of my own free will I wore it. Is its pattern strange to *you*?"

Scrooge trembled more and more.

"Or would you know," pursued the Ghost, "the weight and length of the strong coil you bear yourself? It was full as heavy and as long as this seven Christmas Eves ago. You have labored on it since. It is a ponderous chain!"

Scrooge glanced about him on the floor, in the expectation of finding himself surrounded by some fifty or sixty fathoms of iron cable; but he could see nothing.

"Jacob," he said, imploringly, "old Jacob Marley, tell me more. Speak comfort to me, Jacob!"

"I have none to give," the Ghost replied. "It comes from other regions, Ebenezer Scrooge, and is conveyed by other ministers, to other kinds of men. Nor can I tell you what I would. A very little more is all permitted to me. I cannot rest, I cannot stay, I cannot linger anywhere. My spirit never walked beyond our counting-house—mark me!—in life my spirit never roved beyond the narrow limits of our money-changing hole, and weary journeys lie before me!"

It was a habit with Scrooge, whenever he became thoughtful, to put his hands in his breeches pockets. Pondering on what the Ghost had said, he did so now, but without lifting up his eyes or getting off his knees.

"You must have been very slow about it, Jacob," Scrooge observed, in a business-like manner, though with humility and deference.

"Slow!" the Ghost repeated.

"Seven years dead," mused Scrooge, "and traveling all the time!"

"The whole time," said the Ghost. "No rest, no peace. Incessant torture of remorse."

"You travel fast?" said Scrooge.

"On the wings of the wind," replied the Ghost.

"You might have got over a great quantity of ground in seven years," said Scrooge.

The Ghost, on hearing this, set up another cry, and clanked its chain so hideously in the dead silence of the night that the Ward would have been justified in indicting it for a nuisance.

"Oh, captive, bound and double-ironed!" cried the phantom, "not to know that ages of incessant labor, by immortal creatures, for this earth must pass into eternity before the good of which it is susceptible is all developed. Not to know that any Christian spirit working kindly in its little sphere, whatever it may be, will find its mortal life too short for its vast means of usefulness. Not to know that no space of regret can make amends for one life's opportunity misused! Yet such was I! Oh, such was I!"

"But you were always a good man of business, Jacob," faltered Scrooge, who now began to apply this to himself.

"Business!" cried the Ghost, wringing its hands again. "Mankind was my business. The common welfare was my business; charity, mercy, forbearance, and benevolence were all my business. The dealings of my trade were but a drop of water in the comprehensive ocean of my business!"

It held up its chain at arm's-length, as if that were the cause of all its unavailing grief, and flung it heavily upon the ground again.

"At this time of the rolling year," the Specter said, "I suffer most. Why did I walk through crowds of fellow-beings with my eyes turned down, and never raise them to that blessed Star which led the Wise Men to a poor abode! Were there no poor homes to which its light would have conducted *me*?"

Scrooge was very much dismayed to hear the Specter going on at this rate, and began to quake exceedingly.

"Hear me!" cried the Ghost. "My time is nearly gone."

"I will," said Scrooge. "But don't be hard upon me! Don't be flowery, Jacob, pray!"

"How it is that I appear before you in a shape that you can see, I may not tell. I have sat invisible beside you many and many a day."

It was not an agreeable idea. Scrooge shivered and wiped the perspiration from his brow.

"That is no light part of my penance," pursued the Ghost. "I am here to-night to warn you, that you have yet a chance and hope of escaping my fate. A chance and hope of my procuring, Ebenezer."

"You were always a good friend to me," said Scrooge. "Thank'ee!"

"You will be haunted," resumed the Ghost, "by three spirits."

Scrooge's countenance fell almost as low as the Ghost's had done.

"Is that the chance and hope you mentioned, Jacob?" he demanded, in a faltering voice.

"It is."

"I—I think I'd rather not," said Scrooge.

"Without their visits," said the Ghost, "you cannot hope to shun the path I tread. Expect the first to-morrow, when the bell tolls one."

"Couldn't I take 'em all at once and have it over, Jacob?" hinted Scrooge.

"Expect the second on the next night at the same hour. The third upon the next night when the last stroke of twelve has ceased to vibrate. Look to see me no more; and look that, for your own sake, you remember what has passed between us!"

When it had said these words the Specter took its wrapper from the table and bound it round its head as before. Scrooge knew this by the smart sound its teeth made when the jaws were brought together by the bandage. He ventured to raise his eyes again, and found his supernatural visitor confronting him in an erect attitude, with its chain wound over and about its arm.

The apparition walked backward from him and at every step it took the window raised itself a little, so that when the Specter reached it, it was wide open.

It beckoned Scrooge to approach which he did. When they were within two paces of each other, Marley's Ghost held up its hand, warning him to come no nearer. Scrooge stopped.

Not so much in obedience as in surprise and fear; for on the raising of the hand, he became sensible of confused noises in the air; incoherent sounds of lamentation and regret; wailings inexpressibly sorrowful and self-accusatory. The Specter, after listening for a moment, joined in the mournful dirge, and floated out upon the bleak, dark night.

Scrooge followed to the window, desperate in his curiosity. He looked out.

The air was filled with phantoms, wandering hither and thither in restless haste, and moaning as they went. Every one of them wore chains like Marley's Ghost; some few (they might be guilty governments) were linked together; none were free. Many had been personally known to Scrooge in their lives. He had been quite familiar with one old ghost in a white waistcoat, with a monstrous iron safe attached to its ankle, who cried piteously at being unable to assist a wretched woman with an infant, whom it saw below, upon a door-step. The misery with them all was clearly that they sought to interfere, for good, in human matters, and had lost the power forever.

Whether these creatures faded into mist, or mist enshrouded them, he could not tell. But they and their spirit voices faded together, and the night became as it had been when he walked home.

Scrooge closed the window, and examined the door by which the Ghost had entered. It was double-locked, as he had locked it with his own hands, and the bolts were undisturbed. He tried to say "Humbug!" but stopped at the first syllable. And being—from the emotion he had undergone, or the fatigues of the day, or his glimpse of the invisible world, or the dull conversation of the Ghost, or the lateness of the hour—much in need of repose, went straight to bed without undressing, and fell asleep upon the instant.

STAVE TWO.

THE FIRST OF THE THREE SPIRITS.

When Scrooge awoke it was so dark that, looking out of bed, he could scarcely distinguish the transparent window from the opaque walls of his chamber. He was endeavoring to pierce the darkness with his ferret eyes when the chimes of a neighboring church struck the four quarters. So he listened for the hour.

To his great astonishment the heavy bell went on from six to seven, and from seven to eight, and regularly up to twelve; then stopped. Twelve! It was past two when he went to bed. The clock was wrong. An icicle must have got into the works. Twelve!

He touched the spring of his repeater to correct this most preposterous clock. Its rapid little pulse beat twelve, and stopped.

"Why, it isn't possible," said Scrooge, "that I can have slept through a whole day and far into another night. It isn't possible that anything has happened to the sun, and this is twelve at noon!"

The idea being an alarming one, he scrambled out of bed, and groped his way to the window. He was obliged to rub the frost off with the sleeve of his dressing-gown before he could see anything; and could see very little then. All he could make out was, that it was still very foggy and extremely cold, and that there was no noise of people running to and fro, and making a great stir, as there unquestionably would have been if night had beaten off bright day and taken possession of the world. This was a great relief, because "three days after sight of this First of Exchange pay to Mr. Ebenezer Scrooge or his order," and so forth, would have become a mere United States' security if there were no days to count by.

Scrooge went to bed again and thought and thought, and thought it over and over and over, and could make nothing of it. The more he thought, the more perplexed he was; and the more he endeavored not to think, the more he thought.

Marley's Ghost bothered him exceedingly. Every time he resolved within himself, after mature inquiry, that it was all a dream, his mind flew back again, like a strong spring released to its first position, and presented the same problem to be worked all through, "Was it a dream or not?"

Scrooge lay in this state until the chime had gone three-quarters more, when he remembered, on a sudden, that the Ghost had warned him of a visitation when the bell tolled one. He resolved to lie awake until the hour was passed; and considering that he could no more go to sleep than go to heaven, this was perhaps the wisest resolution in his power.

The quarter was so long that he was more than once convinced he must have sunk into a doze unconsciously, and missed the clock. At length it broke upon his listening ear.

"Ding, dong!"

"A quarter past," said Scrooge, counting.

"Ding, dong!"

"Half-past!" said Scrooge.

"Ding, dong!"

"A quarter to it," said Scrooge.

"Ding, dong!"

"The hour itself," said Scrooge, triumphantly, "and nothing else!"

He spoke before the hour bell sounded, which it now did with a deep, dull, hollow, melancholy ONE. Light flashed up in the room upon the instant, and the curtains of his bed were drawn.

The curtains of his bed were drawn aside, I tell you, by a hand. Not the curtains at his feet, nor the curtains at his back, but those to which his face was addressed. The curtains of his bed were drawn aside; and Scrooge, starting up into a half-recumbent attitude, found himself face to face with the unearthly visitor who drew them, as close to it as I am now to you, and I am standing in the spirit at your elbow.

It was a strange figure—like a child; yet not so like a child as like an old man, viewed through some supernatural medium, which gave him the appearance of having receded from the view, and being diminished to a child's proportions. Its hair, which hung about its neck and down its back, was white as if with age; and yet the face had not a wrinkle in it, and the tenderest bloom was on the skin. The arms were very long and muscular; the hands the same, as if its hold were of uncommon strength. Its legs and feet, most delicately formed, were, like those upper members, bare. It wore a tunic of the purest white; and round its waist was bound a lustrous belt, the sheen of which was beautiful. It held a branch of fresh, green holly in its hand, and in singular contradiction of that wintry emblem, had its dress trimmed with summer flowers. But the strangest thing about it was, that from the crown of its head there sprung a bright, clear jet of light, by which all this was visible; and which was doubtless the occasion of its using, in its duller moments, a great extinguisher for a cap, which it now held under its arm.

Even this, though, when Scrooge looked at it with increasing steadiness, was *not* its strangest quality. For as its belt sparkled and glittered now in one part and now in another, and what was light one instant, at another time was dark, so the figure itself fluctuated in its distinctness; being now a thing with one arm, now with one leg, now with twenty legs, now a pair of legs without a head, now a head without a body, of which dissolving parts no outline would be visible in the dense gloom wherein they melted away. And in the very wonder of this, it would be itself again; distinct and clear as ever.

"Are you the Spirit, sir, whose coming was foretold to me?" asked Scrooge.

"I am!"

The voice was soft and gentle. Singularly low, as if, instead of being so close beside him, it were at a distance.

"Who and what are you?" Scrooge demanded.

"I am the Ghost of Christmas Past."

"Long past?" inquired Scrooge, observant of its dwarfish stature.

"No; your past."

Perhaps Scrooge could not have told anybody why if anybody could have asked him, but he had a special desire to see the Spirit in his cap, and begged him to be covered.

"What!" exclaimed the Ghost, "would you so soon put out, with worldly hands, the light I give? Is it not enough that you are one of those whose passions made this cap, and force me through whole trains of years to wear it low upon my brow!"

Scrooge reverently disclaimed all intention to offend or any knowledge of having willfully "bonneted" the Spirit at any period of his life. He then made bold to inquire what business brought him there.

"Your welfare!" said the Ghost.

Scrooge expressed himself much obliged, but could not help thinking that a night of unbroken rest would have been more conducive to that end. The

Spirit must have heard him thinking, for it said immediately, "Your reclamation, then. Take heed!"

It put out its strong hand as it spoke, and clasped him gently by the arm.

"Rise, and walk with me!"

It would have been in vain for Scrooge to plead that the weather and the hour were not adapted to pedestrian purposes; that the bed was warm, and the thermometer a long way below freezing; that he was clad but lightly in his slippers, dressing-gown, and night-cap; and that he had a cold upon him at that time. The grasp, though gentle as a woman's hand, was not to be resisted. He rose; but finding that the Spirit made towards the window, clasped his robe in supplication.

"I am a mortal," Scrooge remonstrated, "and liable to fall."

"Bear but a touch of my hand *there,*" said the Spirit, laying it upon his heart, "and you shall be upheld in more than this!"

As the words were spoken, they passed through the wall, and stood upon an open country road, with fields on either hand. The city had entirely vanished. Not a vestige of it was to be seen. The darkness and the mist had vanished with it, for it was a clear, cold, winter day, with snow upon the ground.

"Good heaven!" said Scrooge, clasping his hands together as he looked about him. "I was bred in this place. I was a boy here!"

The Spirit gazed upon him mildly. Its gentle touch, though it had been light and instantaneous, appeared still present to the old man's sense of feeling. He was conscious of a thousand odors floating in the air, each one connected with a thousand thoughts, and hopes, and joys, and cares, long, long forgotten!

"Your lip is trembling," said the Ghost. "And what is that upon your cheek?"

Scrooge muttered, with an unusual catching in his voice, that it was a pimple; and begged the Ghost to lead him where he would.

"You recollect the way?" inquired the Spirit.

"Remember it!" cried Scrooge, with fervor; "I could walk it blindfold."

"Strange to have forgotten it for so many years!" observed the Ghost. "Let us go on."

They walked along the road. Scrooge recognizing every gate, and post, and tree, until a little market-town appeared in the distance, with its bridge, its church, and winding river. Some shaggy ponies now were seen trotting towards them with boys upon their backs, who called to other boys in country gigs and carts, driven by farmers. All these boys were in great spirits, and shouted to each other, until the broad fields were so full of merry music that the crisp air laughed to hear it.

"These are but shadows of the things that have been," said the Ghost. "They have no consciousness of us."

The jocund travelers came on; and as they came, Scrooge knew and named them every one. Why was he rejoiced beyond all bounds to see them! Why did his cold eye glisten, and his heart leap up as they went past! Why was he filled with gladness when he heard them give each other Merry Christmas, as they parted at cross-roads and by-ways, for their several homes! What was merry Christmas to Scrooge? Out upon merry Christmas! What good had it ever done to him?

"The school is not quite deserted," said the Ghost. "A solitary child, neglected by his friends, is left there still."

Scrooge said he knew it. And he sobbed.

They left the high-road by a well-remembered lane and soon approached a mansion of dull red brick, with a little weather-cock-surmounted cupola on the roof, and a bell hanging in it. It was a large house, but one of broken fortunes, for the spacious offices were little used, their walls were damp and mossy, their windows broken, and their gates decayed. Fowls clucked and strutted in the stables, and the coach-houses and sheds were overrun with grass. Nor was it more retentive of its ancient state within; for entering the dreary hall, and glancing through the open doors of many rooms, they found them poorly furnished, cold, and vast. There was an earthy savor in the air, a chilly bareness in the place, which associated itself somehow with too much getting up by candle-light, and not too much to eat.

They went, the Ghost and Scrooge, across the hall, to a door at the back of the house. It opened before them, and disclosed a long, bare, melancholy room, made barer still by lines of plain deal forms and desks. At one of these a lonely boy was reading near a feeble fire, and Scrooge sat down upon a form, and wept to see his poor forgotten self as he used to be.

Not a latent echo in the house, not a squeak and scuffle from the mice behind the paneling, not a drip from the half-thawed water-spout in the dull yard behind, not a sigh among the leafless boughs of one despondent poplar, not the idle swinging of an empty store-house door, no, not a clicking in the fire, but fell upon the head of Scrooge with a softening influence, and gave a freer passage to his tears.

The Spirit touched him on the arm, and pointed to his younger self, intent upon his reading. Suddenly a man, in foreign garments—wonderfully real and distinct to look at—stood outside the window, with an axe stuck in his belt, and leading by the bridle an ass laden with wood.

"Why, it's Ali Baba!" Scrooge exclaimed, in ecstasy. "It's dear old honest Ali Baba! Yes, yes, I know! One Christmas time, when yonder solitary child was left here all alone, he *did* come, for the first time, just like that. Poor boy! And Valentine," said Scrooge, "and his wild brother, Orson; there they go! And what's his name, who was put down in his drawers, asleep, at the Gate of Damascus; don't you see him? And the Sultan's Groom turned upside down by the Genii; there he is upon his head! Serve him right. I'm glad of it. What business had *he* to be married to the Princess!"

To hear Scrooge expending all the earnestness of his nature on such subjects, in a most extraordinary voice between laughing and crying, and to see his heightened and excited face, would have been a surprise to his business friends in the city, indeed.

"There's the parrot!" cried Scrooge. "Green body and yellow tail, with a thing like a lettuce growing out of the top of his head; there he is! Poor Robin Crusoe, he called him, when he came home again after sailing round the island. 'Poor Robin Crusoe, where have you been, Robin Crusoe?' The man thought he was dreaming, but he wasn't. It was the parrot, you know. There goes Friday, running for his life to the little creek! Halloa! Hoop! Halloo!"

Then, with a rapidity of transition very foreign to his usual character, he said, in pity for his former self, "Poor boy!" and cried again.

"I wish," Scrooge muttered, putting his hand in his pocket, and looking about him, after drying his eyes with his cuff, "—but it's too late now."

"What is the matter?" asked the Spirit.

"Nothing," said Scrooge. "Nothing. There was a boy singing a Christmas carol at my door last night. I should like to have given him something; that's all."

The Ghost smiled, thoughtfully, and waved its hand, saying as it did so, "Let us see another Christmas!"

Scrooge's former self grew larger at the words, and the room became a little darker and more dirty. The panels shrunk, the windows cracked; fragments of plaster fell out of the ceiling, and the naked laths were shown instead; but how all this was brought about, Scrooge knew no more than you do. He only knew that it was quite correct; that everything had happened so; that there he was, alone again, when all the other boys had gone home for the jolly holidays.

He was not reading now, but walking up and down despairingly. Scrooge looked at the Ghost, and with a mournful shaking of his head, glanced anxiously towards the door.

It opened, and a little girl, much younger than the boy, came darting in, and putting her arms about his neck, and often kissing him, addressed him as her "Dear, dear brother."

"I have come to bring you home, dear brother!" said the child, clapping her tiny hands, and bending down to laugh. "To bring you home, home, home!"

"Home, little Fan?" returned the boy.

"Yes!" said the child, brimful of glee. "Home for good and all. Home, forever and ever. Father is so much kinder than he used to be that home's like heaven! He spoke so gently to me one dear night when I was going to bed, that I was not afraid to ask him once more if you might come home; and he said yes, you should; and sent me in a coach to bring you. And you're to be a man," said the child, opening her eyes, "and are never to come back here; but first, we're to be together all the Christmas long, and have the merriest time in all the world."

"You are quite a woman, little Fan!" exclaimed the boy.

She clapped her hands and laughed, and tried to touch his head; but being too little, laughed again, and stood on tiptoe to embrace him. Then she began to drag him, in her childish eagerness, towards the door; and he, nothing loth to go, accompanied her.

A terrible voice in the hall cried, "Bring down Master Scrooge's box, there!" and in the hall appeared the school-master himself, who glared on Master Scrooge with a ferocious condescension, and threw him into a dreadful state of mind by shaking hands with him. He then conveyed him and his sister into the veriest old well of a shivering best parlor that ever was seen, where the maps upon the wall, and the celestial and terrestrial globes in the windows, were waxy with cold. Here he produced a decanter of curiously light wine and a block of curiously heavy cake, and administered instalments of those dainties to the young people; at the same time sending out a meager servant to offer a glass of "something" to the post-boy, who answered that he thanked the gentleman, but if it was the same tap as he had tasted before, he had rather not. Master Scrooge's trunk being by this time tied onto the top of the chaise, the children bade the school-master good by right willingly, and getting into it drove gayly down the garden sweep; the quick wheels dashing the hoar-frost and snow from off the dark leaves of the evergreens like spray.

"Always a delicate creature, whom a breath might have withered," said the Ghost. "But she had a large heart!"

"So she had," cried Scrooge. "You're right. I will not gainsay it, Spirit. God forbid!"

"She died a woman," said the Ghost, "and had, as I think, children."

"One child," Scrooge returned.

"True," said the Ghost. "Your nephew!"

Scrooge seemed uneasy in his mind, and answered, briefly, "Yes."

Although they had but that moment left the school behind them, they were now in the busy thoroughfares of a city, where shadowy passengers passed and repassed; where shadowy carts and coaches battled for the way, and all the strife and tumult of a real city were. It was made plain enough, by the dressing of the shops, that here, too, it was Christmas time again; but it was evening, and the streets were lighted up.

The Ghost stopped at a certain warehouse door, and asked Scrooge if he knew it.

"Know it!" said Scrooge. "Was I apprenticed here!"

They went in. At sight of an old gentleman in a Welsh wig, sitting behind such a high desk that if he had been two inches taller he must have knocked his head against the ceiling, Scrooge cried in great excitement, "Why, it's old Fezziwig! Bless his heart; it's Fezziwig alive again!"

Old Fezziwig laid down his pen and looked up at the clock, which pointed to the hour of seven. He rubbed his hands; adjusted his capacious waistcoat; laughed all over himself, from his shoes to his organ of benevolence; and called out in a comfortable, oily, rich, fat, jovial voice, "Yo ho, there! Ebenezer! Dick!"

Scrooge's former self, now grown a young man, came briskly in, accompanied by his fellow-'prentice.

"Dick Wilkins, to be sure!" said Scrooge to the Ghost. "Bless me, yes. There he is. He was very much attached to me, was Dick. Poor Dick! Dear, dear!"

"Yo ho, my boys!" said Fezziwig. "No more work to-night. Christmas Eve, Dick. Christmas, Ebenezer! Let's have the shutters up," cried old Fezziwig, with a sharp clap of his hands, "before a man can say Jack Robinson!"

You wouldn't believe how those two fellows went at it! They charged into the street with the shutters—one, two, three—had 'em up in their places—four, five, six—barred 'em and pinned 'em—seven, eight, nine—and came back before you could have got to twelve, panting like race-horses.

"Hilli-ho!" cried old Fezziwig, skipping down from the high desk, with wonderful agility. "Clear away, my lads, and let's have lots of room here! Hilli-ho, Dick! Chirrup, Ebenezer!"

Clear away! There was nothing they wouldn't have cleared away, or couldn't have cleared away, with old Fezziwig looking on. It was done in a minute. Every movable was packed off, as if it were dismissed from public life forevermore, the floor was swept and watered, the lamps were trimmed, fuel was heaped upon the fire; and the warehouse was as snug, and warm, and dry, and bright a ball-room as you would desire to see upon a winter's night.

In came a fiddler with a music-book, and went up to the lofty desk, and made an orchestra out of it, and tuned like fifty stomachaches. In came Mrs. Fezziwig, one vast, substantial smile. In came the three Miss Fezziwigs, beaming and lovable. In came the six young followers whose hearts they broke. In came all the young men and women employed in the business. In came the housemaid, with her cousin, the baker. In came the cook, with her brother's particular friend, the milkman. In came the boy from over the way, who was suspected of not having board enough from his master; trying to hide himself behind the girl from next door but one, who was proved to have had her ears pulled by her mistress. In they all came, one after another; some shyly, some boldly, some gracefully, some awkwardly, some pushing, some pulling; in they all came, anyhow and everyhow. Away they all went, twenty couple at once; hands half round and back again the other way; down the middle and up again; round and round in various stages of affectionate grouping; old top couple always turning up in the wrong place; new top couple starting off again, as soon as they got there; all top couples at last, and not a bottom one to help them! When this result was brought about, old Fezziwig, clapping his hands to stop the dance, cried out, "Well done!" and the fiddler plunged his hot face into a pot of porter especially provided for that purpose. But scorning rest, upon his reappearance, he instantly began again—though there were no dancers yet—as if the other fiddler had been carried home, exhausted, on a shutter, and he were a brand-new man, resolved to beat him out of sight or perish.

There were more dances, and there were forfeits, and more dances, and there was cake, and there was negus, and there was a great piece of cold roast, and there was a great piece of cold boiled, and there were mince-pies, and plenty of beer. But the great effect of the evening came after the roast and boiled, when the fiddler (an artful dog, mind! The sort of man who knew his business better than you or I could have told it him!) struck up "Sir Roger de Coverley." Then old Fezziwig stood out to dance with Mrs. Fezziwig. Top couple, too, with a good, stiff piece of work cut out for them; three or four and twenty pair of partners; people who were not to be trifled with; people who *would* dance, and had no notion of walking.

But if they had been twice as many—ah, four times—old Fezziwig would have been a match for them, and so would Mrs. Fezziwig. As to *her*, she was worthy to be his partner in every sense of the term. If that's not high praise, tell me higher and I'll use it. A positive light appeared to issue from Fezziwig's calves. They shone in every part of the dance like moons. You couldn't have predicted, at any given time, what would have become of them next. And when old Fezziwig and Mrs. Fezziwig had gone all through the dance—advance and retire, both hands to your partner, bow and curtsey, cork-screw, thread-the-needle, and back again to your place—Fezziwig "cut"—cut so deftly that he appeared to wink with his legs, and came up on his feet again without a stagger.

When the clock struck eleven, this domestic ball broke up. Mr. and Mrs. Fezziwig took their stations, one on either side of the door, and shaking hands with every person individually as he or she went out, wished him or her a Merry Christmas. When everybody had retired but the two 'prentices, they did the same to them; and thus the cheerful voices died away, and the lads were left to their beds, which were under a counter in the back shop.

During the whole of this time Scrooge had acted like a man out of his wits. His heart and soul were in the scene, and with his former self. He corroborated everything, remembered everything, enjoyed everything, and underwent the strangest agitation. It was not until now, when the bright faces of his former self and Dick were turned from them, that he remembered the Ghost, and became conscious that it was looking full upon him, while the light upon its head burnt very clear.

"A small matter," said the Ghost, "to make these silly folks so full of gratitude."

"Small!" echoed Scrooge.

The spirit signed to him to listen to the two apprentices, who were pouring out their hearts in praise of Fezziwig; and when he had done so, said, "Why, is it not? He has spent but a few pounds of your mortal money—three or four, perhaps. Is that so much that he deserves this praise?"

"It isn't that," said Scrooge, heated by the remark, and speaking unconsciously like his former, not his latter self. "It isn't that, Spirit. He has the power to render us happy or unhappy; to make our service light or burdensome; a pleasure or a toil. Say that his power lies in words and looks; in things so slight and insignificant that it is impossible to add and count 'em up: what then? The happiness he gives is quite as great as if it cost a fortune."

He felt the Spirit's glance, and stopped.

"What is the matter?" asked the Ghost.

"Nothing particular," said Scrooge.

"Something, I think?" the Ghost insisted.

"No," said Scrooge, "No. I should like to be able to say a word or two to my clerk just now. That's all."

His former self turned down the lamps as he gave utterance to the wish; and Scrooge and the Ghost again stood side by side in the open air.

"My time grows short," observed the Spirit. "Quick!"

This was not addressed to Scrooge, or to any one whom he could see, but it produced an immediate effect. For again Scrooge saw himself. He was older now; a man in the prime of life. His face had not the harsh and rigid lines of later years, but it had begun to wear the signs of care and avarice. There was an eager, greedy, restless motion in the eye, which showed the passion that had taken root, and where the shadow of the growing tree would fall.

He was not alone, but sat by the side of a fair young girl in a mourning dress, in whose eyes there were tears which sparkled in the light that shone out of the Ghost of Christmas Past.

"It matters little," she said, softly. "To you, very little. Another idol has displaced me, and if it can cheer and comfort you in time to come as I would have tried to do, I have no just cause to grieve."

"What idol has displaced you?" he rejoined.

"A golden one."

"This is the even-handed dealing of the world!" he said. "There is nothing on which it is so hard as poverty; and there is nothing it professes to condemn with such severity as the pursuit of wealth!"

"You fear the world too much," she answered, gently. "All your other hopes have merged into the hope of being beyond the chance of its sordid reproach. I have seen your nobler aspirations fall off one by one, until the master-passion, Gain, engrosses you. Have I not?"

"What then?" he retorted. "Even if I have grown so much wiser, what then? I am not changed towards you."

She shook her head.

"Am I?"

"Our contract is an old one. It was made when we were both poor and content to be so, until, in good season, we could improve our worldly fortune by our patient industry. You *are* changed. When it was made, you were another man."

"I was a boy," he said, impatiently.

"Your own feeling tells you that you were not what you are," she returned. "I am. That which promised happiness when we were one in heart, is fraught with misery now that we are two. How often and how keenly I have thought of this, I will not say. It is enough that I *have* thought of it, and can release you."

"Have I ever sought release?"

"In words. No, never."

"In what, then?"

"In a changed nature; in an altered spirit; in another atmosphere of life; another hope as its great end. In everything that made my love of any worth or value in your sight. If this had ever been between us," said the girl, looking mildly, but with steadiness upon him, "tell me, would you seek me out and try to win me now? Ah, no!"

He seemed to yield to the justice of this supposition, in spite of himself. But he said, with a struggle, "You think not."

"I would gladly think otherwise if I could," she answered, "heaven knows! When *I* have learned a truth like this, I know how strong and irresistible it must be. But if you were free to-day, to-morrow, yesterday, can even I believe that you would choose a dowerless girl—you who, in your very confidence with her, weigh everything by gain; or choosing her, if for a moment you were false enough to your one guiding principle to do so, do I not know that your repentance and regret would surely follow? I do; and I release you, with a full heart, for the love of him you once were."

He was about to speak; but with her head turned from him, she resumed. "You may—the memory of what is past half makes me hope you will— have pain in this. A very, very brief time, and you will dismiss the recollection of it gladly, as an unprofitable dream, from which it happened well that you awoke. May you be happy in the life you have chosen!"

She left him and they parted.

"Spirit!" said Scrooge, "show me no more! Conduct me home. Why do you delight to torture me?"

"One shadow more!" exclaimed the Ghost.

"No more!" cried Scrooge. "No more. I don't wish to see it. Show me no more!"

But the relentless Ghost pinioned him in both his arms, and forced him to observe what happened next.

They were in another scene and place; a room, not very large or handsome, but full of comfort. Near to the winter fire sat a beautiful young girl, so like that last that Scrooge believed it was the same, until he saw *her*, now a comely matron, sitting opposite her daughter. The noise in this room was perfectly tumultuous, for there were more children there than Scrooge in his agitated state of mind could count; and unlike the celebrated herd in the poem, there were not forty children conducting themselves like one, but every child was conducting itself like forty. The consequences were uproarious beyond belief; but no one seemed to care; on the contrary, the mother and daughter laughed heartily, and enjoyed it very much; and the latter, soon beginning to mingle in the sports, got pillaged by the young brigands most ruthlessly. What would I not have given to be one of them. Though I never could have been so rude, no, no! I wouldn't for the wealth of all the world have crushed that braided hair and torn it down; and for the precious little shoe, I wouldn't have plucked it off, God bless my soul! to save my life. As to measuring her waist in sport, as they did, bold young brood, I couldn't have done it; I should have expected my arm to have grown round it for a punishment, and never come straight again. And yet I should have dearly liked, I own, to have touched her lips; to have questioned her, that she might have opened them; to have looked upon the lashes of her downcast eyes, and never raised a blush; to have let loose waves of hair, an inch of which would be a keepsake beyond price; in short, I should have liked, I do confess, to have had the lightest license of a child, and yet to have been man enough to know its value.

But now a knocking at the door was heard, and such a rush immediately ensued that she, with laughing face and plundered dress, was borne towards it, the center of a flushed and boisterous group, just in time to greet the father, who came home attended by a man laden with Christmas toys and presents. Then the shouting and the struggling, and the onslaught that was made on the defenseless porter! The scaling him with chairs for ladders to dive into his pockets, despoil him of brown paper parcels, hold on tight by his cravat, hug him round his neck, pommel his back, and kick his legs in irrepressible affection! The shouts of wonder and delight with which the development of every package was received! The terrible announcement that the baby had been taken in the act of putting a doll's frying-pan into his mouth, and was more than suspected of having swallowed a fictitious turkey glued on a wooden platter! The immense relief of finding this a false alarm! The joy, and gratitude, and ecstasy! They are all indescribable alike. It is enough that by degrees the children and their emotions got out of the parlor, and by one stair at a time, up to the top of the house, where they went to bed, and so subsided.

And now Scrooge looked on more attentively than ever, when the master of the house, having his daughter leaning fondly on him, sat down with her and her mother at his own fireside; and when he thought that such another creature, quite as graceful and as full of promise, might have called him father, and been a springtime in the haggard winter of his life, his sight grew very dim indeed.

"Belle," said the husband, turning to his wife, with a smile, "I saw an old friend of yours this afternoon."

"Who was it?"

"Guess!"

"How can I? Tut, don't I know," she added, in the same breath, laughing as he laughed. "Mr. Scrooge."

"Mr. Scrooge it was. I passed his office window, and as it was not shut up and he had a candle inside, I could scarcely help seeing him. His partner lies upon the point of death, I hear, and there he sat alone. Quite alone in the world, I do believe."

"Spirit!" said Scrooge, in a broken voice, "remove me from this place."

"I told you these were shadows of the things that have been," said the Ghost. "That they are what they are, do not blame me!"

"Remove me!" Scrooge exclaimed, "I cannot bear it!"

He turned upon the Ghost, and seeing that it looked upon him with a face, in which in some strange way there were fragments of all the faces it had shown him, wrestled with it.

"Leave me! Take me back. Haunt me no longer!"

In the struggle, if that can be called a struggle in which the Ghost with no visible resistance on its own part was undisturbed by any effort of its adversary, Scrooge observed that its light was burning high and bright, and dimly connecting that with its influence over him, he seized the extinguisher-cap, and by a sudden action pressed it down upon its head.

The Spirit dropped beneath it, so that the extinguisher covered its whole form; but though Scrooge pressed it down with all his force, he could not hide the light which streamed from under it in an unbroken flood upon the ground.

He was conscious of being exhausted, and overcome by an irresistible drowsiness; and further, of being in his own bedroom. He gave the cap a parting squeeze, in which his hand relaxed, and had barely time to reel to bed before he sank into a heavy sleep.

STAVE THREE.

THE SECOND OF THE THREE SPIRITS.

Awaking in the middle of a prodigiously tough snore, and sitting up in bed to get his thoughts together, Scrooge had no occasion to be told that the bell was again upon the stroke of one. He felt that he was restored to consciousness in the right nick of time, for the especial purpose of holding a conference with the second messenger despatched to him through Jacob Marley's intervention. But finding that he turned uncomfortably cold when he began to wonder which of his curtains this new specter would draw back, he put them every one aside with his own hands, and lying down again, established a sharp lookout all round the bed. For he wished to challenge the Spirit on the moment of its appearance, and did not wish to be taken by surprise, and made nervous.

Gentlemen of the free-and-easy sort, who plume themselves on being acquainted with a move or two, and being usually equal to the time of day, express the wide range of their capacity for adventure by observing that they are good for anything from pitch-and-toss to manslaughter, between which opposite extremes, no doubt, there lies a tolerably wide and comprehensive range of subjects. Without venturing for Scrooge quite as hardily as this, I don't mind calling on you to believe that he was ready for a good, broad field of strange appearances, and that nothing between a baby and rhinoceros would have astonished him very much.

Now, being prepared for almost anything, he was not by any means prepared for nothing; and consequently, when the bell struck one, and no shape appeared, he was taken with a violent fit of trembling. Five minutes, ten minutes, a quarter of an hour went by, yet nothing came. All this time he lay upon his bed, the very core and center of a blaze of ruddy light which streamed upon it when the clock proclaimed the hour, and which, being only light, was more alarming than a dozen ghosts, as he was powerless to make out what it meant, or would be at, and was sometimes apprehensive that he might be that very moment an interesting case of spontaneous combustion, without having the consolation of knowing it. At last, however, he began to think—as you or I would have thought at first, for it is always the person not in the predicament who knows what ought to have been done in it, and would unquestionably have done it, too—at last, I say, he began to think that the source and secret of this ghostly light might be in the adjoining room, from whence, on further tracing it, it seemed to shine. This idea taking full possession of his mind, he got up softly and shuffled in his slippers to the door.

The moment Scrooge's hand was on the lock, a strange voice called him by his name, and bade him enter. He obeyed.

It was his own room. There was no doubt about that. But it had undergone a surprising transformation. The walls and ceiling were so hung with living green that it looked a perfect grove, from every part of which bright gleaming berries glistened. The crisp leaves of holly, mistletoe, and ivy reflected back the light as if so many little mirrors had been scattered there, and such a mighty blaze went roaring up the chimney as that dull petrifaction of a hearth had never known in Scrooge's time, or Marley's, or for many and many a winter season gone. Heaped up on the floor, to form a kind of throne, were turkeys, geese, game, poultry, brawn, great joints of meat, sucking pigs, long wreaths of sausages, mince-pies, plum-puddings, barrels of oysters, red-hot chestnuts, cherry-cheeked apples, juicy oranges, luscious pears, immense twelfth-cakes, and seething bowls of punch, that made the chamber dim with their delicious steam. In easy state upon this couch, there sat a jolly giant, glorious to see, who bore a glowing torch, in shape not unlike Plenty's horn, and held it up, high up, to shed its light on Scrooge as he came peeping round the door.

"Come in!" exclaimed the Ghost. "Come in! and know me better, man!"

Scrooge entered, timidly, and hung his head before this Spirit. He was not the dogged Scrooge he had been, and though the Spirit's eyes were clear and kind, he did not like to meet them.

"I am the Ghost of Christmas Present," said the Spirit. "Look upon me!"

Scrooge reverently did so. It was clothed in one simple green robe, or mantle, bordered with white fur. This garment hung so loosely on the figure that its capacious breast was bare, as if disdaining to be warded or concealed by any artifice. Its feet, observable beneath the ample folds of the garment, were also bare, and on its head it wore no other covering than a holly wreath, set here and there with shining icicles. Its dark brown curls were long and free—free as its genial face, its sparkling eye, its open hand, its cheery voice, its unconstrained demeanor, and its joyful air. Girded round its middle was an antique scabbard, but no sword was in it, and the ancient sheath was eaten up with rust.

"You have never seen the like of me before!" exclaimed the Spirit.

"Never!" Scrooge made answer to it.

"Have never walked forth with the younger members of my family, meaning (for I am very young) my elder brothers born in these later years?" pursued the Phantom.

"I don't think I have," said Scrooge. "I am afraid I have not. Have you had many brothers, Spirit?"

"More than eighteen hundred," said the Ghost.

"A tremendous family to provide for!" muttered Scrooge.

The Ghost of Christmas Present rose.

"Spirit," said Scrooge, submissively, "conduct me where you will. I went forth last night on compulsion, and I learnt a lesson which is working now. To-night, if you have aught to teach me, let me profit by it."

"Touch my robe!"

Scrooge did as he was told, and held it fast.

Holly, mistletoe, red berries, ivy, turkeys, geese, game, poultry, brawn, meat, pigs, sausages, oysters, pies, puddings, fruit, and punch all vanished instantly. So did the room, the fire, the ruddy glow, the hour of night, and they stood in the city streets on Christmas morning, where (for the weather was severe) the people made a rough, but brisk and not unpleasant kind of music in scraping the snow from the pavement in front of their dwellings, and from the tops of their houses, whence it was mad delight to the boys to see it come plumping down into the road below, and splitting into artificial little snow-storms.

The house fronts looked black enough, and the windows blacker, contrasting with the smooth, white sheet of snow upon the roofs, and with the dirtier snow upon the ground; which last deposit had been ploughed up in deep furrows by the heavy wheels of carts and wagons—furrows that crossed and re-crossed each other hundreds of times where the great streets branched off, and made intricate channels hard to trace in the thick, yellow mud and icy water. The sky was gloomy and the shortest streets were choked up with a dingy mist, half thawed, half frozen, whose heavier particles descended in a shower of sooty atoms, as if all the chimneys in Great Britain had, by one consent, caught fire, and were blazing away to their dear hearts' content. There was nothing very cheerful in the climate of the town, and yet was there an air of cheerfulness abroad that the clearest summer air and brightest summer sun might have endeavored to diffuse in vain. For the people who were shoveling away on the housetops were jovial and full of glee; calling out to one another from the parapets, and now and then exchanging a facetious snowball—better-natured missile far than many a wordy jest—laughing heartily if it went right, and not less heartily if it went wrong. The poulterers' shops were still half open, and the fruiterers' were radiant in their glory. There were great, round, pot-bellied baskets of chestnuts, shaped like the waistcoats of jolly old gentlemen, lolling at the doors, and tumbling out into the street in their apoplectic opulence. There were ruddy, brown-faced, broad-girthed Spanish onions, shining in the fatness of their growth like Spanish friars, and winking from their shelves in wanton slyness at the girls as they went by, and glanced demurely at the hung-up mistletoe. There were pears and apples clustered high in blooming pyramids; there were bunches of grapes made, in the shopkeepers' benevolence, to dangle from conspicuous hooks, that people's mouths might water gratis as they passed; there were piles of filberts, mossy and brown, recalling, in their fragrance, ancient walks among the woods, and pleasant shufflings ankle deep through withered leaves; there were Norfolk Biffins, squab and swarthy, setting off the yellow of the oranges and lemons, and in the great compactness of their juicy persons, urgently entreating and beseeching to be carried home in paper bags and eaten after dinner. The very gold and silver fish, set forth among these choice fruits in a bowl, though members of a dull and stagnant blooded race, appeared to know that there was something going on, and to a fish went gasping round and round their little world in slow and passionless excitement.

The grocers'! oh the grocers'! nearly closed, with perhaps two shutters down, or one; but through those gaps such glimpses! It was not alone that the scales descending on the counter made a merry sound, or that the twine and roller parted company so briskly, or that the canisters were rattled up and down like juggling tricks, or even that the blended scents of tea and coffee were so grateful to the nose, or even that the raisins were so plentiful and pure, the almonds so extremely white, the sticks of cinnamon so long and straight, the other spices so delicious, the candied fruits so caked and spotted with molten sugar as to make the coldest lookers-on feel faint and subsequently bilious. Nor was it that the figs were moist and pulpy, or that the French plums blushed in modest tartness from their highly decorated boxes, or that everything was good to eat and in its Christmas dress; but the customers were all so hurried and so eager in the hopeful promise of the day, that they tumbled up against each other at the door, crashing their wicker baskets wildly, and left their purchases upon the counter, and came running back to fetch them, and committed hundreds of the like mistakes, in the best humor possible; while the grocer and his people were so frank and fresh that the polished hearts with which they fastened their aprons behind might have been their own, worn outside for general inspection, and for Christmas daws to peck at if they chose.

But soon the steeples called good people all to church and chapel, and away they came, flocking through the streets in their best clothes, and with their gayest faces. At the same time there emerged from scores of by-streets, lanes, and nameless turnings, innumerable people, carrying their dinners to the bakers' shops. The sight of these poor revelers appeared to interest the Spirit very much, for he stood with Scrooge beside him in a baker's doorway, and taking off the covers as their bearers passed, sprinkled incense on their dinners from his torch. And it was a very uncommon kind of torch, for once or twice when there were angry words between some dinner-carriers who had jostled each other, he shed a few drops of water on them from it, and their good humor was restored directly, for they said, it was a shame to quarrel upon Christmas Day. And so it was! God love it, so it was!

In time the bells ceased and the bakers were shut up; and yet there was a genial shadowing forth of all these dinners and the progress of their cooking in the thawed blotch of wet above each baker's oven, where the pavement smoked as if the stones were cooking, too.

"Is there a peculiar flavor in what you sprinkle from your torch?" asked Scrooge.

"There is; my own."

"Would it apply to any kind of dinner on this day?" asked Scrooge.

"To any kindly given. To a poor one most."

"Why to a poor one most?" asked Scrooge.

"Because it needs it most."

"Spirit," said Scrooge, after a moment's thought, "I wonder you, of all the beings in the many worlds about us, should desire to cramp these people's opportunities of innocent enjoyment."

"I!" cried the Spirit.

"You would deprive them of their means of dining every seventh day, often the only day on which they can be said to dine at all," said Scrooge, "wouldn't you?"

"I!" cried the Spirit.

"You seek to close these places on the seventh day," said Scrooge, "and it comes to the same thing."

"*I* seek!" exclaimed the Spirit.

"Forgive me if I am wrong. It has been done in your name, or at least in that of your family," said Scrooge.

"There are some upon this earth of yours," returned the Spirit, "who lay claim to know us, and who do their deeds of passion, pride, ill-will, hatred, envy, bigotry, and selfishness in our name, who are as strange to us and all our kith and kin as if they had never lived. Remember that, and charge their doings on themselves, not us."

Scrooge promised that he would, and they went on, invisible, as they had been before, into the suburbs of the town. It was a remarkable quality of the Ghost (which Scrooge had observed at the baker's), that notwithstanding his gigantic size, he could accommodate himself to any place with ease, and that he stood beneath a low roof quite as gracefully and like a supernatural creature as it was possible he could have done in any lofty hall.

And perhaps it was the pleasure the good Spirit had in showing off this power of his, or else it was his own kind, generous, hearty nature, and his sympathy with all poor men, that led him straight to Scrooge's clerk's; for there he went, and took Scrooge with him, holding to his robe; and on the threshold of the door the Spirit smiled, and stopped to bless Bob Cratchit's dwelling with the sprinklings of his torch. Think of that! Bob had but fifteen "Bob" a-week himself; he pocketed on Saturdays but fifteen copies of his Christian name; and yet the Ghost of Christmas Present blessed his four-roomed house!

Then up rose Mrs. Cratchit, Cratchit's wife, dressed out but poorly in a twice-turned gown, but brave in ribbons, which are cheap and make a goodly show for sixpence; and she laid the cloth, assisted by Belinda Cratchit, second of her daughters, also brave in ribbons; while Master Peter Cratchit plunged a fork into the saucepan of potatoes, and getting the corners of his monstrous shirt collar (Bob's private property, conferred upon his son and heir in honor of the day) into his mouth, rejoiced to find himself so gallantly attired, and yearned to show his linen in the fashionable parks. And now two smaller Cratchits, boy and girl, came tearing in, screaming that outside the baker's they had smelt the goose and known it for their own, and basking in luxurious thoughts of sage and onion, these young Cratchits danced about the table, and exalted Master Peter Cratchit to the skies, while he (not proud, although his collars nearly choked him) blew the fire until the slow potatoes bubbling up knocked loudly at the saucepan lid to be led out and peeled.

"What has ever got your precious father then?" said Mrs. Cratchit. "And your brother, Tiny Tim! And Martha warn't as late last Christmas Day by half an hour."

"Here's Martha, mother!" said a girl, appearing as she spoke.

"Here's Martha, mother!" cried the two young Cratchits. "Hurrah! There's *such* a goose, Martha!"

"Why, bless your heart alive, my dear, how late you are!" said Mrs. Cratchit, kissing her a dozen times, and taking off her shawl and bonnet for her with officious zeal.

"We'd a deal of work to finish up last night," replied the girl, "and had to clear away this morning, mother!"

"Well, never mind so long as you are come," said Mrs. Cratchit. "Sit ye down before the fire, my dear, and have a warm, Lord bless ye!"

"No, no! There's father coming," cried the two young Cratchits, who were everywhere at once. "Hide, Martha, hide!"

So Martha hid herself, and in came little Bob, the father, with at least three feet of comforter, exclusive of the fringe, hanging down before him, and his threadbare clothes darned up and brushed to look seasonable, and Tiny Tim upon his shoulder. Alas for Tiny Tim, he bore a little crutch and had his limbs supported by an iron frame!

"Why, where's our Martha?" cried Bob Cratchit, looking round.

"Not coming," said Mrs. Cratchit.

"Not coming!" said Bob, with a sudden declension in his high spirits, for he had been Tim's blood horse all the way from church, and had come home rampant; "not coming upon Christmas Day!"

Martha didn't like to see him disappointed, if it were only a joke, so she came out prematurely from behind the closet door and ran into his arms, while the two young Cratchits hustled Tiny Tim and bore him off into the wash-house, that he might hear the pudding singing in the copper.

"And how did little Tim behave?" asked Mrs. Cratchit, when she had rallied Bob on his credulity, and Bob had hugged his daughter to his heart's content.

"As good as gold," said Bob, "and better. Somehow he gets thoughtful, sitting by himself so much, and thinks the strangest things you ever heard. He told me coming home that he hoped the people saw him in the church, because he was a cripple, and it might be pleasant to them to remember upon Christmas Day who made lame beggars walk and blind men see."

Bob's voice was tremulous when he told them this, and trembled more when he said that Tiny Tim was growing strong and hearty.

His active little crutch was heard upon the floor, and back came Tiny Tim before another word was spoken, escorted by his brother and sister to his stool before the fire, and while Bob, turning up his cuffs—as if, poor fellow, they were capable of being made more shabby—compounded some hot mixture in a jug with gin and lemons, and stirred it round and round and put it on the hob to simmer, Master Peter and the two ubiquitous young Cratchits went to fetch the goose, with which they soon returned in high procession.

Such a bustle ensued that you might have thought a goose the rarest of all birds; a feathered phenomenon, to which a black swan was a matter of course—and in truth it was something very like it in that house. Mrs. Cratchit made the gravy (ready beforehand in a little saucepan) hissing hot; Master Peter mashed the potatoes with incredible vigor; Miss Belinda sweetened up the apple sauce; Martha dusted the hot plates; Bob took Tiny Tim beside him in a tiny corner at the table; the two young Cratchits set chairs for everybody, not forgetting themselves, and mounting guard upon their posts, crammed spoons into their mouths, lest they should shriek for goose before their turn came to be helped. At last the dishes were set on, and grace was said. It was succeeded by a breathless pause, as Mrs. Cratchit, looking slowly all along the carving-knife, prepared to plunge it in the breast; but when she did, and when the long-expected gush of stuffing issued forth, one murmur of delight arose all round the board, and even

Tiny Tim, excited by the two young Cratchits, beat on the table with the handle of his knife, and feebly cried Hurrah!

There never was such a goose. Bob said he didn't believe there ever was such a goose cooked. Its tenderness and flavor, size and cheapness, were the themes of universal admiration. Eked out by apple sauce and mashed potatoes it was a sufficient dinner for the whole family; indeed, as Mrs. Cratchit said with great delight (surveying one small atom of a bone upon the dish), they hadn't ate it all at last! Yet every one had had enough, and the youngest Cratchits in particular were steeped in sage and onion to the eyebrows! But now, the plates being changed by Miss Belinda, Mrs. Cratchit left the room alone—too nervous to bear witnesses—to take the pudding up and bring it in.

Suppose it should not be done enough! Suppose it should break in turning out! Suppose somebody should have got over the wall of the back yard and stolen it while they were merry with the goose—a supposition at which the two young Cratchits became livid! All sorts of horrors were supposed.

Hallo! A great deal of steam! The pudding was out of the copper. A smell like a washing-day! That was the cloth. A smell like an eating-house and a pastry-cook's next door to each other, with a laundress's next door to that! That was the pudding. In half a minute Mrs. Cratchit entered—flushed, but smiling proudly—with the pudding, like a speckled canon-ball, so hard and firm, blazing in half of half a-quartern of ignited brandy, and bedight with Christmas holly stuck into the top.

Oh, a wonderful pudding! Bob Cratchit said, and calmly, too, that he regarded it as the greatest success achieved by Mrs. Cratchit since their marriage. Mrs. Cratchit said that now the weight was off her mind, she would confess she had had her doubts about the quantity of flour. Everybody had something to say about it, but nobody said or thought it was at all a small pudding for a large family. It would have been flat heresy to do so. Any Cratchit would have blushed to hint at such a thing.

At last the dinner was all done, the cloth was cleared, the hearth swept, and the fire made up. The compound in the jug being tasted and considered perfect, apples and oranges were put upon the table, and a shovelful of chestnuts on the fire. Then all the Cratchit family drew round the hearth, in what Bob Cratchit called a circle, meaning half a one, and at Bob Cratchit's elbow stood the family display of glass: two tumblers and a custard-cup without a handle.

These held the hot stuff from the jug, however, as well as golden goblets would have done; and Bob served it out with beaming looks, while the chestnuts on the fire sputtered and cracked noisily. Then Bob proposed: "A Merry Christmas to us all, my dears. God bless us!"

Which all the family re-echoed.

"God bless us every one!" said Tiny Tim, the last of all.

He sat very close to his father's side upon his little stool. Bob held his withered little hand in his, as if he loved the child, and wished to keep him by his side, and dreaded that he might be taken from him.

"Spirit," said Scrooge, with an interest he had never felt before, "tell me if Tiny Tim will live."

"I see a vacant seat," replied the Ghost, "in the poor chimney-corner, and a crutch without an owner, carefully preserved. If these shadows remain unaltered by the future, the child will die."

"No, no," said Scrooge. "Oh, no, kind Spirit! say he will be spared."

"If these shadows remain unaltered by the future, none other of my race," returned the Ghost, "will find him here. What then? If he be like to die, he had better do it, and decrease the surplus population."

Scrooge hung his head to hear his own words quoted by the Spirit, and was overcome with penitence and grief.

"Man," said the Ghost, "if man you be in heart, not adamant, forbear that wicked cant until you have discovered What the surplus is, and Where is it. Will you decide what men shall live, what men shall die? It may be that, in the sight of heaven, you are more worthless and less fit to live than millions like this poor man's child. Oh, God, to hear the insect on the leaf pronouncing on the too much life among his hungry brothers in the dust!"

Scrooge bent before the Ghost's rebuke, and trembling, cast his eyes upon the ground. But he raised them speedily on hearing his own name.

"Mr. Scrooge!" said Bob; "I'll give you Mr. Scrooge, the founder of the feast!"

"The founder of the feast, indeed!" cried Mrs. Cratchit, reddening. "I wish I had him here. I'd give him a piece of my mind to feast upon, and I hope he'd have a good appetite for it."

"My dear," said Bob, "the children! Christmas Day."

"It should be Christmas Day, I am sure," said she, "on which one drinks the health of such an odious, stingy, hard, unfeeling man as Mr. Scrooge. You know he is, Robert! Nobody knows it better than you do, poor fellow!"

"My dear," was Bob's mild answer, "Christmas Day."

"I'll drink his health for your sake and the day's," said Mrs. Cratchit, "not for his. Long life to him! A Merry Christmas and a Happy New Year! He'll be very merry and very happy, I have no doubt!"

The children drank the toast after her. It was the first of their proceedings which had no heartiness. Tiny Tim drank it last of all, but he didn't care twopence for it. Scrooge was the Ogre of the family. The mention of his name cast a dark shadow on the party, which was not dispelled for full five minutes.

After it had passed away, they were ten times merrier than before, from the mere relief of Scrooge the baleful being done with. Bob Cratchit told them how he had a situation in his eye for Master Peter, which would bring in, if obtained, full five-and-sixpence weekly. The two young Cratchits laughed tremendously at the idea of Peter's being a man of business; and Peter himself looked thoughtfully at the fire from between his collars, as if he were deliberating what particular investments he should favor when he came into the receipt of that bewildering income. Martha, who was a poor apprentice at a milliner's, then told them what kind of work she had to do, and how many hours she worked at a stretch, and how she meant to lie abed to-morrow morning for a good long rest; to-morrow being a holiday she passed at home. Also how she had seen a countess and a lord some days before, and how the lord "was much about as tall as Peter"; at which Peter pulled up his collars so high that you couldn't have seen his head if you had been there. All this time the chestnuts and the jug went round and round, and by and by they had a song, about a lost child traveling in the snow, from Tiny Tim, who had a plaintive little voice, and sang it very well indeed.

There was nothing of high mark in this. They were not a handsome family; they were not well dressed; their shoes were far from being waterproof; their clothes were scanty; and Peter might have known, and very likely did, the inside of a pawnbroker's. But they were happy, grateful, pleased with one another, and contented with the time; and when they faded and looked happier yet in the bright sprinklings of the Spirit's torch at parting, Scrooge had his eye upon them, and especially on Tiny Tim, until the last.

By this time it was getting dark and snowing pretty heavily, and as Scrooge and the Spirit went along the streets, the brightness of the roaring fires in kitchens, parlors, and all sorts of rooms was wonderful. Here the flickering of the blaze showed preparations for a cozy dinner, with hot plates baking through and through before the fire, and deep red curtains, ready to be drawn to shut out cold and darkness. There all the children of the house were running out into the snow to meet their married sisters, brothers, cousins, uncles, aunts, and be the first to greet them. Here, again, were shadows on the windowblind of guests assembling; and there a group of handsome girls, all hooded and fur-booted, and all chattering at once, tripped lightly off to some near neighbor's house, where, woe upon the single man who saw them enter—artful witches, well they knew it—in a glow!

But if you had judged from the numbers of people on their way to friendly gatherings, you might have thought that no one was at home to give them welcome when they got there, instead of every house expecting company, and piling up its fires half-chimney high. Blessings on it, how the Ghost exulted. How it bared its breadth of breast, and opened its capacious palm, and floated on, outpouring, with a generous hand, its bright and harmless mirth on everything within its reach! The very lamplighter, who ran on before, dotting the dusky street with specks of light, and who was dressed to spend the evening somewhere, laughed out loudly as the Spirit passed, though little kenned the lamplighter that he had any company but Christmas!

And now, without a word of warning from the Ghost, they stood upon a bleak and desert moor, where monstrous masses of rude stone were cast about, as though it were the burial-place of giants, and water spread itself wheresoever it listed, or would have done so, but for the frost that held it prisoner; and nothing grew but moss and furze, and coarse, rank grass. Down in the west the setting sun had left a streak of fiery red, which glared upon the desolation for an instant like a sullen eye, and frowning lower, lower, lower yet, was lost in the thick gloom of darkest night.

"What place is this?" asked Scrooge.

"A place where miners live, who labor in the bowels of the earth," returned the Spirit. "But they know me. See!"

A light shone from the window of a hut, and swiftly they advanced towards it. Passing through the wall of mud and stone, they found a cheerful company assembled round a glowing fire. An old, old man and woman, with their children and their children's children, and another generation beyond that, all decked out gayly in their holiday attire. The old man, in a voice that seldom rose above the howling of the wind upon the barren waste, was singing them a Christmas song—it had been a very old song when he was a boy—and from time to time they all joined in the chorus. So surely as they raised their voices, the old man got quite blithe and loud, and so surely as they stopped, his vigor sank again.

The Spirit did not tarry here, but bade Scrooge hold his robe, and passing on above the moor, sped—whither? Not to sea? To sea. To Scrooge's horror, looking back, he saw the last of the land, a frightful range of rocks behind them, and his ears were deafened by the thundering of water, as it rolled and roared, and raged among the dreadful caverns it had worn, and fiercely tried to undermine the earth.

Built upon a dismal reef of sunken rocks, some league or so from shore, on which the waters chafed and dashed, the wild year through, there stood a solitary lighthouse. Great heaps of seaweed clung to its base, and storm birds—born of the wind one might suppose, as seaweed of the water—rose and fell about it, like the waves they skimmed.

But even here, two men who watched the light had made a fire, that through the loophole in the thick stone wall shed out a ray of brightness on the awful sea. Joining their horny hands over the rough table at which they sat, they wished each other Merry Christmas in their can of grog; and one of them—the elder, too, with his face all damaged and scarred with hard weather, as the figurehead of an old ship might be—struck up a sturdy song that was like a gale in itself.

Again the Ghost sped on, above the black and heaving sea—on, on—until, being far away, as he told Scrooge, from any shore, they lighted on a ship. They stood beside the helmsman at the wheel, the lookout in the bow, the officers who had the watch—dark, ghostly figures in their several stations; but every man among them hummed a Christmas tune, or had a Christmas thought, or spoke below his breath to his companion of some bygone Christmas Day, with homeward hopes belonging to it. And every man on board, waking or sleeping, good or bad, had had a kinder word for another on that day than on any day in the year; and had shared to some extent in its festivities; and had remembered those he cared for at a distance; and had known that they delighted to remember him.

It was a great surprise to Scrooge, while listening to the moaning of the wind, and thinking what a solemn thing it was to move on through the lonely darkness over an unknown abyss, whose depths were secrets as profound as death, it was a great surprise to Scrooge, while thus engaged to hear a hearty laugh. It was a much greater surprise to Scrooge to recognize it as his own nephew's and to find himself in a bright, dry, gleaming room, with the Spirit standing smiling by his side, and looking at that same nephew with approving affability!

"Ha, ha!" laughed Scrooge's nephew. "Ha, ha, ha!"

If you should happen, by any unlikely chance, to know a man more blest in a laugh than Scrooge's nephew, all I can say is, I should like to know him, too. Introduce him to me, and I'll cultivate his acquaintance.

It is a fair, even-handed, noble adjustment of things, that while there is infection in disease and sorrow, there is nothing in the world so irresistibly contagious as laughter and good humor. When Scrooge's nephew laughed in this way—holding his sides, rolling his head, and twisting his face into the most extravagant contortions—Scrooge's niece, by marriage, laughed as heartily as he, and their assembled friends being not a bit behindhand, roared out lustily.

"Ha, ha! Ha, ha, ha, ha!"

"He said that Christmas was a humbug, as I live!" cried Scrooge's nephew. "He believed it, too!"

"More shame for him, Fred!" said Scrooge's niece, indignantly. Bless those women; they never do anything by halves, they are always in earnest.

She was very pretty, exceedingly pretty. With a dimpled, surprised-looking, capital face; a ripe little mouth that seemed made to be kissed, as no doubt it was; all kinds of good little dots about her chin that melted into one another when she laughed; and the sunniest pair of eyes you ever saw in any little creature's head. Altogether she was what you would have called provoking, you know; but satisfactory, too. Oh, perfectly satisfactory.

"He's a comical old fellow," said Scrooge's nephew, "that's the truth, and not so pleasant as he might be. However, his offenses carry their own punishment, and I have nothing to say against him."

"I'm sure he is very rich, Fred," hinted Scrooge's niece. "At least you always tell *me* so."

"What of that, my dear!" said Scrooge's nephew. "His wealth is of no use to him. He don't do any good with it. He don't make himself comfortable with it. He hasn't the satisfaction of thinking—ha, ha, ha!—that he is ever going to benefit us with it."

"I have no patience with him," observed Scrooge's niece. Scrooge's niece's sisters and all the other ladies, expressed the same opinion.

"Oh, I have!" said Scrooge's nephew. "I am sorry for him; I couldn't be angry with him if I tried. Who suffers by his ill whims! Himself, always. Here, he takes it into his head to dislike us, and he won't come and dine with us. What's the consequence? He don't lose much of a dinner."

"Indeed, I think he loses a very good dinner," interrupted Scrooge's niece. Everybody else said the same, and they must be allowed to have been competent judges, because they had just had dinner, and with the dessert upon the table, were clustered round the fire, by lamplight.

"Well, I'm very glad to hear it," said Scrooge's nephew, "because I haven't great faith in these young housekeepers. What do *you* say, Topper?"

Topper had clearly got his eye upon one of Scrooge's niece's sisters, for he answered that a bachelor was a wretched outcast, who had no right to express an opinion on the subject. Whereas Scrooge's niece's sister—the plump one with the lace tucker; not the one with the roses—blushed.

"Do go on, Fred," said Scrooge's niece, clapping her hands. "He never finishes what he begins to say; he is such a ridiculous fellow!"

Scrooge's nephew reveled in another laugh, and as it was impossible to keep the infection off—though the plump sister tried hard to do it with aromatic vinegar—his example was unanimously followed.

"I was only going to say," said Scrooge's nephew, "that the consequence of his taking a dislike to us, and not making merry with us, is, as I think, that he loses some pleasant moments which could do him no harm. I am sure he loses pleasanter companions than he can find in his own thoughts, either in his moldy old office or his dusty chambers. I mean to give him the same chance every year, whether he likes it or not, for I pity him. He may rail at Christmas till he dies, but he can't help thinking better of it—I defy him—if he finds me going there, in good temper, year after year, and saying, Uncle Scrooge, how are you? If it only puts him in the vein to leave his poor clerk fifty pounds, *that's* something, and I think I shook him yesterday."

It was their turn to laugh now, at the notion of his shaking Scrooge. But being thoroughly good-natured, and not much caring what they laughed at so that they laughed at any rate, he encouraged them in their merriment and passed the bottle joyously.

After tea, they had some music, for they were a musical family, and knew what they were about, when they sung a Glee or Catch, I can assure you, especially Topper, who could growl away in the bass like a good one, and never swell the large veins in his forehead, or get red in the face over it. Scrooge's niece played well upon the harp, and played among other tunes a simple little air (a mere nothing—you might learn to whistle it in two minutes), which had been familiar to the child who fetched Scrooge from the boarding-school, as he had been reminded by the Ghost of Christmas Past. When the strain of music sounded, all the things that Ghost had shown him came upon his mind, he softened more and more, and thought that if he could have listened to it often years ago, he might have cultivated the kindness of life for his own happiness with his own hands, without resorting to the sexton's spade that buried Jacob Marley.

But they didn't devote the whole evening to music. After a while they played at forfeits, for it is good to be children sometimes, and never better than at Christmas, when its mighty Founder was a child himself. Stop! There was first a game at blind-man's buff. Of course there was. And I no more believe that Topper was really blind than I believe he had eyes in his boots. My opinion is that it was a done thing between him and Scrooge's nephew, and that the Ghost of Christmas Present knew it. The way he went after that plump sister in the lace tucker was an outrage on the credulity of human nature. Knocking down the fire-irons, tumbling over the chairs, bumping against the piano, smothering himself among the curtains, wherever she went, there went he! He always knew where the plump sister was. He wouldn't catch anybody else. If you had fallen up against him (as some of them did on purpose), he would have made a feint of endeavoring to seize you, which would have been an affront to your understanding, and would instantly have sidled off in the direction of the plump sister. She often cried out that it wasn't fair, and it really was not. But when at last he caught her; when, in spite of all her silken rustlings, and her rapid flutterings past him, he got her into a corner whence there was no escape; then his conduct was the most execrable. For his pretending not to know her, his pretending that it was necessary to touch her head-dress, and further to assure himself of her identity by pressing a certain ring upon her finger, and a certain chain about her neck, was vile, monstrous! No doubt she told him her opinion of it, when, another blind man being in office, they were so very confidential together behind the curtains.

Scrooge's niece was not one of the blind-man's buff party, but was made comfortable with a large chair and a footstool, in a snug corner, where the Ghost and Scrooge were close behind her. But she joined in the forfeits and loved her love to admiration with all the letters of the alphabet. Likewise at the game of How, When, and Where, she was very great, and to the secret joy of Scrooge's nephew, beat her sisters hollow, though they were sharp girls, too, as Topper could have told you. There might have been twenty people there, young and old, but they all played, and so did Scrooge, for wholly forgetting, in the interest he had in what was going on, that his voice made no sound in their ears, he sometimes came out with his guess quite loud, and very often guessed quite right, too; for the sharpest needle, best Whitechapel, warranted not to cut in the eye, was not sharper than Scrooge; blunt as he took it in his head to be.

The Ghost was greatly pleased to find him in this mood, and looked upon him with such favor that he begged like a boy to be allowed to stay until the guests departed. But this the Spirit said could not be done.

"Here is a new game," said Scrooge. "One half-hour, Spirit, only one!"

It was a game called Yes and No, where Scrooge's nephew had to think of something, and the rest must find out what; he only answering to their questions yes or no, as the case was. The brisk fire of questioning to which he was exposed elicited from him that he was thinking of an animal, a live animal, rather a disagreeable animal, a savage animal, an animal that growled and grunted sometimes, and talked sometimes, and lived in London, and walked about the streets, and wasn't made a show of, and wasn't led by anybody, and didn't live in a menagerie, and was never killed in a market, and was not a horse, or an ass, or a cow, or a bull, or a tiger, or a dog, or a pig, or a cat, or a bear. At every fresh question that was put to him, this nephew burst into a fresh roar of laughter, and was so inexpressibly tickled that he was obliged to get up off the sofa and stamp. At last the plump sister, falling into a similar state, cried out, "I have found it out! I know what it is, Fred! I know what it is!"

"What is it?" cried Fred.

"It's your Uncle Scro-o-o-o-oge!"

Which it certainly was. Admiration was the universal sentiment, though some objected that the reply to "Is it a bear?" ought to have been "Yes," inasmuch as an answer in the negative was sufficient to have diverted their thoughts from Mr. Scrooge, supposing they had ever had any tendency that way.

"He has given us plenty of merriment, I am sure," said Fred, "and it would be ungrateful not to drink his health. Here is a glass of mulled wine ready to our hand at the moment; and I say, 'Uncle Scrooge!'"

"Well! Uncle Scrooge!" they cried.

"A Merry Christmas and a Happy New Year to the old man, whatever he is!" said Scrooge's nephew. "He wouldn't take it from me, but may he have it, nevertheless. Uncle Scrooge!"

Uncle Scrooge had imperceptibly become so gay and light of heart that he would have pledged the unconscious company in return, and thanked them in an inaudible speech if the Ghost had given him time. But the whole scene passed off in the breath of the last word spoken by his nephew, and he and the Spirit were again upon their travels.

Much they saw, and far they went, and many homes they visited, but always with a happy end. The Spirit stood beside sick beds, and they were cheerful; on foreign lands, and they were close at home; by struggling men, and they were patient in their greater hope; by poverty, and it was rich. In almshouse, hospital, and jail, in misery's every refuge, where vain man in his little brief authority had not made fast the door and barred the Spirit out, he left his blessing and taught Scrooge his precepts.

It was a long night, if it were only a night; but Scrooge had his doubts of this, because the Christmas holidays appeared to be condensed into the space of time they passed together. It was strange, too, that while Scrooge remained unaltered in his outward form, the Ghost grew older, clearly older. Scrooge had observed this change, but never spoke of it until they left a children's Twelfth-Night party, when, looking at the Spirit as they stood together in an open place, he noticed that its hair was gray.

"Are spirits' lives so short?" asked Scrooge.

"My life upon this globe is very brief," replied the Ghost. "It ends to-night."

"To-night!" cried Scrooge.

"To-night at midnight. Hark! The time is drawing near."

The chimes were ringing the three-quarters past eleven at that moment.

"Forgive me if I am not justified in what I ask," said Scrooge, looking intently at the Spirit's robe, "but I see something strange, and not belonging to yourself, protruding from your skirts. Is it a foot or a claw?"

"It might be a claw, for the flesh there is upon it," was the Spirit's sorrowful reply. "Look here."

From the foldings of its robe it brought two children, wretched, abject, frightful, hideous, miserable. They knelt down at its feet, and clung upon the outside of its garment.

"Oh, man! look here. Look, look down here!" exclaimed the Ghost.

They were a boy and girl. Yellow, meager, ragged, scowling, wolfish, but prostrate, too, in their humility. Where graceful youth should have filled their features out and touched them with its freshest tints, a stale and shriveled hand, like that of age, had pinched and twisted them, and pulled them into shreds. Where angels might have sat enthroned, devils lurked and glared out menacing. No change, no degradation, no perversion of humanity in any grade, through all the mysteries of wonderful creation, has monsters half so horrible and dread.

Scrooge started back, appalled. Having them shown to him in this way, he tried to say they were fine children, but the words choked themselves rather than be parties to a lie of such enormous magnitude.

"Spirit, are they yours?" Scrooge could say no more.

"They are man's," said the Spirit, looking down upon them, "and they cling to me, appealing from their fathers. This boy is Ignorance. This girl is Want. Beware them both, and all of their degree, but most of all beware this boy, for on his brow I see that written which is Doom, unless the writing be erased. Deny it!" cried the Spirit, stretching out its hand towards the city.

"Slander those who tell it ye! Admit it for your factious purposes, and make it worse. And abide the end!"

"Have they no refuge or resource?" cried Scrooge.

"Are there no prisons?" said the Spirit, turning on him for the last time with his own words. "Are there no workhouses?"

The bell struck twelve.

Scrooge looked about him for the Ghost, and saw it not. As the last stroke ceased to vibrate, he remembered the prediction of old Jacob Marley, and lifting up his eyes, beheld a solemn Phantom, draped and hooded, coming like a mist along the ground towards him.

STAVE FOUR.

THE LAST OF THE SPIRITS.

The Phantom slowly, gravely, silently approached. When it came near him, Scrooge bent down upon his knee; for in the very air through which this Spirit moved it seemed to scatter gloom and mystery.

It was shrouded in a deep, black garment, which concealed its head, its face, its form, and left nothing of it visible save one outstretched hand. But for this it would have been difficult to detach its figure from the night, and separate it from the darkness by which it was surrounded.

He felt that it was tall and stately when it came beside him, and that its mysterious presence filled him with a solemn dread. He knew no more, for the Spirit neither spoke nor moved.

"I am in the presence of the Ghost of Christmas Yet to Come?" said Scrooge.

The Spirit answered not, but pointed onward with its hand.

"You are about to show me shadows of the things that have not happened, but will happen in the time before us," Scrooge pursued. "Is that so, Spirit?"

The upper portion of the garment was contracted for an instant in its folds, as if the Spirit had inclined its head. That was the only answer he received.

Although well used to ghostly company by this time, Scrooge feared the silent shape so much that his legs trembled beneath him, and he found that he could hardly stand when he prepared to follow it. The Spirit paused a moment, as observing his condition, and giving him time to recover.

But Scrooge was all the worse for this. It thrilled him with a vague uncertain horror to know that behind the dusky shroud there were ghostly eyes intently fixed upon him, while he, though he stretched his own to the utmost, could see nothing but a spectral hand and one great heap of black.

"Ghost of the Future!" he exclaimed, "I fear you more than any specter I have seen. But as I know your purpose is to do me good, and as I hope to live to be another man from what I was, I am prepared to bear you company, and do it with a thankful heart. Will you not speak to me?"

It gave him no reply. The hand was pointed straight before them.

"Lead on!" said Scrooge. "Lead on! The night is waning fast, and it is precious time to me, I know. Lead on, Spirit!"

The Phantom moved away as it had come towards him. Scrooge followed in the shadow of its dress, which bore him up, he thought, and carried him along.

They scarcely seemed to enter the city, for the city rather seemed to spring up about them and encompass them of its own act. But there they were in the heart of it, on 'Change, amongst the merchants, who hurried up and down, and chinked the money in their pockets, and conversed in groups, and looked at their watches, and trifled thoughtfully with their great gold seals, and so forth, as Scrooge had seen them often.

The Spirit stopped beside one little knot of business men. Observing that the hand was pointed to them, Scrooge advanced to listen to their talk.

"No," said a great fat man with a monstrous chin, "I don't know much about it, either way. I only know he's dead."

"When did he die?" inquired another.

"Last night, I believe."

"Why, what was the matter with him?" asked a third, taking a vast quantity of snuff out of a very large snuff-box. "I thought he'd never die."

"God knows," said the first, with a yawn.

"What has he done with his money?" asked a red-faced gentleman with a pendulous excrescence on the end of his nose, that shook like the gills of a turkey-cock.

"I haven't heard," said the man with the large chin, yawning again. "Left it to his company, perhaps. He hasn't left it to *me*. That's all I know."

This pleasantry was received with a general laugh.

"It's likely to be a very cheap funeral," said the same speaker; "for upon my life I don't know of anybody to go to it. Suppose we make up a party and volunteer?"

"I don't mind going if a lunch is provided," observed the gentleman with the excrescence on his nose. "But I must be fed, if I make one."

Another laugh.

"Well, I am the most disinterested among you, after all," said the first speaker, "for I never wear black gloves, and I never eat lunch. But I'll offer to go, if anybody else will. When I come to think of it, I'm not at all sure that I wasn't his most particular friend, for we used to stop and speak whenever we met. By-by!"

Speakers and listeners strolled away and mixed with other groups. Scrooge knew the men, and looked towards the Spirit for an explanation.

The Phantom glided on into a street. Its finger pointed to two persons meeting. Scrooge listened again, thinking that the explanation might lie here.

He knew these men, also, perfectly. They were men of business, very wealthy, and of great importance. He had made a point always of standing well in their esteem, in a business point of view; that is, strictly in a business point of view.

"How are you?" said one.

"How are you?" returned the other.

"Well!" said the first. "Old Scratch has got his own at last, hey?"

"So I am told," returned the second. "Cold, isn't it?"

"Seasonable for Christmas time. You're not a skater, I suppose?"

"No, no. Something else to think of. Good morning!"

Not another word. That was their meeting, their conversation, and their parting.

Scrooge was at first inclined to be surprised that the Spirit should attach importance to conversations apparently so trivial, but feeling assured that they must have some hidden purpose, he set himself to consider what it was likely to be. They could scarcely be supposed to have any bearing on the death of Jacob, his old partner, for that was Past, and this Ghost's province was the Future. Nor could he think of any one immediately connected with himself to whom he could apply them. But nothing doubting that to whomsoever they applied they had some latent moral for his own improvement, he resolved to treasure up every word he heard and everything he saw, and especially to observe the shadow of himself when it appeared. For he had an expectation that the conduct of his future self would give him the clue he missed, and would render the solution of these riddles easy.

He looked about in that very place for his own image, but another man stood in his accustomed corner, and though the clock pointed to his usual time of day for being there, he saw no likeness of himself among the multitudes that poured in through the porch. It gave him little surprise, however, for he had been revolving in his mind a change of life, and thought and hoped he saw his new-born resolutions carried out in this.

Quiet and dark beside him stood the Phantom, with its outstretched hand. When he roused himself from his thoughtful quest, he fancied from the turn of the hand, and its situation in reference to himself, that the unseen eyes were looking at him keenly. It made him shudder and feel very cold.

They left the busy scene and went into an obscure part of the town where Scrooge had never penetrated before, although he recognized its situation and its bad repute. The ways were foul and narrow, the shops and houses wretched, the people half-naked, drunken, slipshod, ugly. Alleys and archways, like so many cesspools, disgorged their offenses of smell, and dirt, and life upon the straggling streets, and the whole quarter reeked with crime, with filth, and misery.

Far in this den of infamous resort there was a low-browed, beetling shop below a pent-house roof, where iron, old rags, bottles, bones, and greasy offal, were bought. Upon the floor within were piled up heaps of rusty keys, nails, chains, hinges, files, scales, weights, and refuse iron of all kinds. Secrets that few would like to scrutinize were bred and hidden in mountains of unseemly rags, masses of corrupted fat, and sepulchers of bones. Sitting in among the wares he dealt in, by a charcoal stove made of old bricks, was a gray-haired rascal, nearly seventy years of age, who had screened himself from the cold air without by a frowsy curtaining of miscellaneous tatters hung upon a line, and smoked his pipe in all the luxury of calm retirement.

Scrooge and the Phantom came into the presence of this man just as a woman with a heavy bundle slunk into the shop. But she had scarcely entered when another woman, similarly laden, came in too, and she was closely followed by a man in faded black, who was no less startled by the sight of them than they had been upon the recognition of each other. After a short period of blank astonishment, in which the old man with the pipe had joined them, they all three burst into a laugh.

"Let the charwoman alone to be the first!" cried she who had entered first. "Let the laundress alone to be the second, and let the under-taker's man alone to be the third. Look here, old Joe, here's a chance! If we haven't all three met here without meaning it!"

"You couldn't have met in a better place," said old Joe, removing his pipe from his mouth. "Come into the parlor. You were made free of it long ago, you know, and the other two an't strangers. Stop till I shut the door of the shop. Ah! How it skreeks! There an't such a rusty bit of metal in the place as its own hinges, I believe, and I'm sure there's no such old bones here as mine. Ha, ha! We're all suitable to our calling, we're well matched. Come into the parlor. Come into the parlor."

The parlor was the space behind the screen of rags. The old man raked the fire together with an old stair-rod, and having trimmed his smoky lamp (for it was night) with the stem of his pipe, put it in his mouth again.

While he did this, the woman who had already spoken threw her bundle on the floor and sat down in a flaunting manner on a stool, crossing her elbows on her knees, and looking with a bold defiance at the other two.

"What odds then! What odds, Mrs. Dilber?" said the woman. "Every person has a right to take care of themselves. *He* always did."

"That's true, indeed!" said the laundress. "No man more so."

"Why, then, don't stand staring as if you was afraid, woman; who's the wiser? We're not going to pick holes in each other's coats, I suppose?"

"No, indeed!" said Mrs. Dilber and the man together. "We should hope not."

"Very well, then!" cried the woman. "That's enough. Who's the worse for the loss of a few things like these? Not a dead man, I suppose."

"No, indeed," said Mrs. Dilber, laughing.

"If he wanted to keep 'em after he was dead, a wicked old screw," pursued the woman, "why wasn't he natural in his lifetime? If he had been, he'd have had somebody to look after him when he was struck with death, instead of lying gasping out his last there, alone, by himself."

"It's the truest word that ever was spoke," said Mrs. Dilber. "It's a judgment on him."

"I wish it was a little heavier judgment," replied the woman, "and it should have been, you depend upon it, if I could have laid my hands on anything else. Open that bundle, old Joe, and let me know the value of it. Speak out plain. I'm not afraid to be the first nor afraid for them to see it. We knew pretty well that we were helping ourselves before we met here, I believe. It's no sin. Open the bundle, Joe."

But the gallantry of her friends would not allow of this, and the man in faded black, mounting the breach first, produced *his* plunder. It was not extensive. A seal or two, a pencil-case, a pair of sleeve-buttons, and a brooch of no great value, were all. They were severally examined and appraised by old Joe, who chalked the sums he was disposed to give for each upon the wall, and added them up into a total when he found there was nothing more to come.

"That's your account," said Joe, "and I wouldn't give another sixpence if I was to be boiled for not doing it. Who's next?"

Mrs. Dilber was next. Sheets and towels, a little wearing apparel, two old-fashioned silver teaspoons, a pair of sugar-tongs, a few boots. Her account was stated on the wall in the same manner.

"I always give too much to ladies. It's a weakness of mine, and that's the way I ruin myself," said old Joe. "That's your account. If you asked me for another penny and made it an open question, I'd repent of being so liberal and knock off half-a-crown."

"And now undo *my* bundle, Joe," said the first woman.

Joe went down on his knees for the greater convenience of opening it, and having unfastened a great many knots, dragged out a large and heavy roll of some dark stuff.

"What do you call this?" said Joe. "Bed-curtains!"

"Ah," returned the woman, laughing and leaning forward on her crossed arms, "bed-curtains!"

"You don't mean to say you took 'em down, rings an all, with him lying there?" said Joe.

"Yes I do," replied the woman. "Why not?"

"You were born to make your fortune," said Joe, "and you'll certainly do it."

"I certainly sha'n't hold my hand, when I can get anything in it by reaching it out, for the sake of such a man as he was, I promise you, Joe," returned the woman, coolly. "Don't drop that oil upon the blankets, now."

"His blankets?" asked Joe.

"Whose else's do you think?" replied the woman. "He isn't likely to take cold without 'em, I dare say."

"I hope he didn't die of anything catching? Eh?" said old Joe, stopping in his work and looking up.

"Don't you be afraid of that," returned the woman. "I an't so fond of his company that I'd loiter about him for such things if he did. Ah! you may look through that shirt till your eyes ache, but you won't find a hole in it, nor a threadbare place. It's the best he had, and a fine one, too. They'd have wasted it, if it hadn't been for me."

"What do you call wasting of it?" asked old Joe.

"Putting it on him to be buried in, to be sure," replied the woman, with a laugh. "Somebody was fool enough to do it, but I took it off again. If calico an't good enough for such a purpose, it isn't good enough for anything. It's quite as unbecoming to the body. He can't look uglier than he did in that one."

Scrooge listened to this dialogue in horror. As they sat grouped about their spoil in the scanty light afforded by the old man's lamp, he viewed them with a detestation and disgust which could hardly have been greater, though they had been obscene demons, marketing the corpse itself.

"Ha, ha!" laughed the same woman, when old Joe, producing a flannel bag with money in it, told out their several gains upon the ground. "This is the end of it, you see! He frightened every one away from him when he was alive, to profit us when he was dead! Ha, ha, ha!"

"Spirit!" said Scrooge, shuddering from head to foot. "I see, I see. The case of this unhappy man might be my own. My life tends that way now. Merciful heaven, what is this!"

He recoiled in terror, for the scene had changed, and now he almost touched a bed—a bare, uncurtained bed—on which, beneath a ragged sheet there lay a something covered up, which, though it was dumb, announced itself in awful language.

The room was very dark, too dark to be observed with any accuracy, though Scrooge glanced round it, in obedience to a secret impulse, anxious to know what kind of room it was. A pale light rising in the outer air, fell straight upon the bed, and on it, plundered and bereft, unwatched, unwept, uncared for, was the body of this man.

Scrooge glanced toward the Phantom. Its steady hand was pointed to the head. The cover was so carelessly adjusted that the slightest raising of it, the motion of a finger upon Scrooge's part, would have disclosed the face. He thought of it, felt how easy it would be to do, and longed to do it, but had no more power to withdraw the veil than to dismiss the specter at his side.

Oh cold, cold, rigid, dreadful Death, set up thine altar here, and dress it with such terrors as thou hast at thy command, for this is thy dominion! But of the loved, revered, and honored head, thou canst not turn one hair to thy dread purposes, or make one feature odious. It is not that the hand is heavy and will fall down when released, it is not that the heart and pulse are still, but that the hand was open, generous, and true; the heart brave, warm, and tender; and the pulse a man's. Strike, Shadow, strike! And see his good deeds springing from the wound, to sow the world with life immortal!

No voice pronounced these words in Scrooge's ears, and yet he heard them when he looked upon the bed. He thought if this man could be raised up now, what would be his foremost thoughts? Avarice, hard-dealing, griping cares? They have brought him to a rich end, truly!

He lay in the dark, empty house with not a man, a woman, or a child to say that he was kind to me in this or that, and for the memory of one kind word I will be kind to him. A cat was tearing at the door, and there was a sound of gnawing rats beneath the hearthstone. What *they* wanted in the room of death, and why they were so restless and disturbed, Scrooge did not dare to think.

"Spirit," he said, "this is a fearful place. In leaving it, I shall not leave its lesson, trust me. Let us go!"

Still the Ghost pointed with an unmoved finger to the head.

"I understand you," Scrooge returned, "and I would do it, if I could. But I have not the power, Spirit. I have not the power."

Again it seemed to look upon him.

"If there is any person in the town who feels emotion caused by this man's death," said Scrooge quite agonized, "show that person to me, Spirit, I beseech you!"

The Phantom spread its dark robe before him for a moment like a wing, and withdrawing it, revealed a room by daylight, where a mother and her children were.

She was expecting some one, and with anxious eagerness, for she walked up and down the room, started at every sound, looked out from the window, glanced at the clock, tried but in vain to work with her needle, and could hardly bear the voices of the children in their play.

At length the long-expected knock was heard. She hurried to the door and met her husband, a man whose face was careworn and depressed, though he was young. There was a remarkable expression in it now, a kind of serious delight, of which he felt ashamed and which he struggled to repress.

He sat down to the dinner that had been hoarding for him by the fire, and when she asked him faintly what news (which was not until after a long silence), he appeared embarrassed how to answer.

"Is it good," she said, "or bad?"—to help him.

"Bad," he answered.

"We are quite ruined?"

"No; there is hope yet, Caroline."

"If *he* relents," she said, amazed, "there is! Nothing is past hope, if such a miracle has happened."

"He is past relenting," said her husband. "He is dead."

She was a mild and patient creature, if her face spoke truth, but she was thankful in her soul to hear it, and she said so, with clasped hands. She prayed forgiveness the next moment, and was sorry, but the first was the emotion of her heart.

"What the half-drunken woman whom I told you of last night said to me when I tried to see him and obtain a week's delay, and what I thought was a mere excuse to avoid me, turns out to have been quite true. He was not only very ill, but dying then."

"To whom will our debt be transferred?"

"I don't know. But before that time we shall be ready with the money, and even though we were not, it would be a bad fortune indeed to find so merciless a creditor in his successor. We may sleep to-night with light hearts, Caroline!"

Yes; soften it as they would, their hearts were lighter. The children's faces, hushed and clustered round to hear what they so little understood, were brighter, and it was a happier house for this man's death! The only emotion that the Ghost could show him, caused by the event, was one of pleasure.

"Let me see some tenderness connected with a death," said Scrooge; "or that dark chamber, Spirit, which we left just now will be forever present to me."

The Ghost conducted him through several streets familiar to his feet, and as they went along, Scrooge looked here and there to find himself, but nowhere was he to be seen. They entered poor Bob Cratchit's house, the dwelling he had visited before, and found the mother and children seated round the fire.

Quiet; very quiet. The noisy little Cratchits were as still as statues in one corner, and sat looking up at Peter, who had a book before him; the mother and her daughters were engaged in sewing. But surely they were very quiet!

"'And He took a child, and set him in the midst of them.'"

Where had Scrooge heard those words? He had not dreamed them. The boy must have read them out, as he and the Spirit crossed the threshold. Why did he not go on?

The mother laid her work upon the table, and put her hand up to her face.

"The color hurts my eyes," she said.

The color? Ah, poor Tiny Tim!

"They're better now again," said Cratchit's wife. "It makes them weak by candlelight, and I wouldn't show weak eyes to your father when he comes home for the world. It must be near his time."

"Past it rather," Peter answered, shutting up his book. "But I think he has walked a little slower than he used, these few last evenings, mother."

They were very quiet again. At last she said, and in a steady, cheerful voice, that only faltered once, "I have known him walk with—I have known him walk with Tiny Tim upon his shoulder, very fast indeed."

"And so have I!" cried Peter; "often."

"And so have I!" exclaimed another. So had all.

"But he was very light to carry," she resumed, intent upon her work, "and his father loved him so that it was no trouble; no trouble. And there is your father at the door!"

She hurried out to meet him, and little Bob in his comforter—he had need of it, poor fellow—came in. His tea was ready for him on the hob, and they all tried who should help him to it most. Then the two young Cratchits got up on his knees and laid each child a little cheek against his face, as if they said, "Don't mind it, father; don't be grieved!"

Bob was very cheerful with them, and spoke pleasantly to all the family. He looked at the work upon the table, and praised the industry and speed of Mrs. Cratchit and the girls. They would be done long before Sunday he said.

"Sunday! You went to-day, then, Robert?" said his wife.

"Yes, my dear," returned Bob. "I wish you could have gone. It would have done you good to see how green a place it is. But you'll see it often. I promised him that I would walk there on a Sunday. My little, little child!" cried Bob. "My little child!"

He broke down all at once. He couldn't help it. If he could have helped it he and his child would have been farther apart perhaps than they were.

He left the room and went upstairs into the room above, which was lighted cheerfully, and hung with Christmas. There was a chair set loose beside the child and there were signs of some one having been there lately. Poor Bob sat down in it, and when he had thought a little and composed himself, he kissed the little face. He was reconciled to what had happened, and went down again quite happy.

They drew about the fire and talked; the girls and mother working still. Bob told them of the extraordinary kindness of Mr. Scrooge's nephew, whom he had scarcely seen but once, and who, meeting him in the street that day, and seeing that he looked a little—"just a little down you know," said Bob, inquired what had happened to distress him. "On which," said Bob, "for he is the pleasantest-spoken gentleman you ever heard, I told him. 'I am heartily sorry for it, Mr. Cratchit,' he said, 'and heartily sorry for your good wife.' By the by, how he ever knew *that*, I don't know."

"Knew what, my dear?"

"Why, that you were a good wife," replied Bob.

"Everybody knows that!" said Peter.

"Very well observed, my boy!" cried Bob. "I hope they do. 'Heartily sorry,' he said, 'for your good wife. If I can be of service to you in any way,' he said, giving me his card, 'that's where I live. Pray come to me.' Now, it wasn't," cried Bob, "for the sake of anything he might be able to do for us, so much as for his kind way, that this was quite delightful. It really seemed as if he had known our Tiny Tim, and felt with us."

"I'm sure he's a good soul!" said Mrs. Cratchit.

"You would be surer of it, my dear," returned Bob, "if you saw and spoke to him. I shouldn't be at all surprised—mark what I say!—if he got Peter a better situation."

"Only hear that, Peter," said Mrs. Cratchit.

"And then," cried one of the girls, "Peter will be keeping company with some one, and setting up for himself."

"Get along with you!" retorted Peter, grinning.

"It's just likely as not," said Bob, "one of these days; though there's plenty of time for that, my dear. But, however and whenever we part from one another, I am sure we shall none of us forget poor Tiny Tim—shall we—or this first parting that there was among us?"

"Never, father!" cried they all.

"And I know," said Bob, "I know, my dears, that when we recollect how patient and how mild he was, although he was a little, little child, we shall not quarrel easily among ourselves and forget poor Tiny Tim in doing it."

"No, never, father!" they all cried again.

"I am very happy," said little Bob; "I am very happy!"

Mrs. Cratchit kissed him, his daughters kissed him, the two young Cratchits kissed him, and Peter and himself shook hands. Spirit of Tiny Tim, thy childish essence was from God.

"Specter," said Scrooge, "something informs me that our parting moment is at hand. I know it, but I know not how. Tell me what man that was whom we saw lying dead?"

The Ghost of Christmas Yet to Come conveyed him, as before—though at a different time, he thought, indeed, there seemed no order in these latter visions, save that they were in the future—into the resorts of business men, but showed him not himself. Indeed, the Spirit did not stay for anything, but went straight on, as to the end just now desired, until besought by Scrooge to tarry for a moment.

"This court," said Scrooge, "through which we hurry now, is where my place of occupation is, and has been for a length of time. I see the house. Let me behold what I shall be in days to come!"

The Spirit stopped, the hand was pointed elsewhere.

"The house is yonder," Scrooge exclaimed. "Why do you point away?"

The inexorable finger underwent no change.

Scrooge hastened to the window of his office and looked in. It was an office still, but not his. The furniture was not the same, and the figure in the chair was not himself. The Phantom pointed as before.

He joined it once again, and wondering why and whither he had gone, accompanied it until they reached an iron gate. He paused to look round before entering.

A churchyard. Here, then, the wretched man whose name he had now to learn lay underneath the ground. It was a worthy place: walled in by houses; overrun by grass and weeds, the growth of vegetation's death, not life; choked up with too much burying; fat with replete appetite. A worthy place!

The Spirit stood among the graves, and pointed down to one. He advanced towards it, trembling. The Phantom was exactly as it had been, but he dreaded that he saw new meaning in its solemn shape.

"Before I draw nearer to that stone to which you point," said Scrooge, "answer me one question. Are these the shadows of the things that will be, or are they shadows of things that may be only?"

Still the Ghost pointed downward to the grave by which it stood.

"Men's courses will foreshadow certain ends, to which, if persevered in, they must lead," said Scrooge; "but if the course be departed from, the ends will change. Say it is thus with what you show me!"

The Spirit was immovable as ever.

Scrooge crept towards it, trembling as he went, and following the finger, read upon the stone of the neglected grave his own name, EBENEZER SCROOGE.

"Am *I* that man who lay upon the bed?" he cried, upon his knees.

The finger pointed from the grave to him, and back again.

"No, Spirit! Oh, no, no!"

The finger still was there.

"Spirit!" he cried, tight clutching at its robe, "hear me! I am not the man I was. I will not be the man I must have been but for this intercourse. Why show me this, if I am past all hope!"

For the first time the hand appeared to shake.

"Good Spirit," he pursued, as down upon the ground he fell before it, "your nature intercedes for me, and pities me. Assure me that I yet may change these shadows you have shown me, by an altered life!"

The kind hand trembled.

"I will honor Christmas in my heart, and try to keep it all the year. I will live in the Past, the Present, and the Future. The Spirits of all three shall strive within me. I will not shut out the lessons that they teach. Oh, tell me I may sponge away the writing on this stone!"

In his agony he caught the spectral hand. It sought to free itself, but he was strong in his entreaty, and detained it. The Spirit, stronger yet, repulsed him.

Holding up his hands in a last prayer to have his fate reversed, he saw an alteration in the Phantom's hood and dress. It shrunk, collapsed, and dwindled down into a bedpost.

STAVE FIVE.

THE END OF IT.

Yes, and the bedpost was his own. The bed was his own. The room was his own. Best and happiest of all, the time before him was his own, to make amends in!

"I will live in the Past, the Present, and the Future!" Scrooge repeated, as he scrambled out of bed. "The spirits of all three shall strive within me. Oh, Jacob Marley! Heaven and the Christmas time be praised for this! I say it on my knees, old Jacob, on my knees!"

He was so fluttered and so glowing with his good intentions that his broken voice would scarcely answer to his call. He had been sobbing violently in his conflict with the Spirit, and his face was wet with tears.

"They are not torn down," cried Scrooge, folding one of his bed-curtains in his arms, "they are not torn down, rings and all. They are here—I am here—the shadows of the things that would have been may be dispelled. They will be! I know they will!"

His hands were busy with his garments all this time, turning them inside out, putting them on upside down, tearing them, mislaying them, making them parties to every kind of extravagance.

"I don't know what to do!" cried Scrooge, laughing and crying in the same breath, and making a perfect Laocoön of himself with his stockings. "I am as light as a feather, I am as happy as an angel, I am as merry as a school-boy. I am as giddy as a drunken man. A Merry Christmas to everybody! A Happy New Year to all the world. Hallo here! Whoop! Hallo!"

He had frisked into the sitting-room, and was now standing there, perfectly winded.

"There's the saucepan that the gruel was in!" cried Scrooge, starting off again, and going round the fireplace. "There's the door by which the Ghost of Jacob Marley entered! There's the corner where the Ghost of Christmas Present sat! There's the window where I saw the wandering Spirits! It's all right, it's all true, it all happened. Ha, ha, ha!"

Really, for a man who had been out of practice for so many years, it was a splendid laugh, a most illustrious laugh. The father of a long, long line of brilliant laughs!

"I don't know what day of the month it is!" said Scrooge. "I don't know how long I've been among the spirits. I don't know anything. I'm quite a baby. Never mind. I don't care. I'd rather be a baby. Hallo! Whoop! Hallo here!"

He was checked in his transports by the churches ringing out the lustiest peals he had ever heard. Clash, clang, hammer; ding, dong, bell. Bell, dong, ding; hammer, clang, clash! Oh, glorious, glorious!

Running to the window, he opened it and put out his head. No fog, no mist; clear, bright, jovial, stirring, cold; cold, piping for the blood to dance to—golden sunlight; heavenly sky; sweet fresh air; merry bells. Oh, glorious! Glorious!

"What's to-day?" cried Scrooge, calling downward to a boy in Sunday clothes, who perhaps had loitered in to look about him.

"Eh?" returned the boy, with all his might of wonder.

"What's to-day, my fine fellow?" said Scrooge.

"To-day!" replied the boy. "Why, Christmas Day."

"It's Christmas Day!" said Scrooge to himself. "I haven't missed it. The Spirits have done it all in one night. They can do anything they like. Of course they can. Of course they can. Hallo, my fine fellow!"

"Hallo!" returned the boy.

"Do you know the poulterer's, in the next street but one, at the corner?" Scrooge inquired.

"I should hope I did," replied the lad.

"An intelligent boy!" said Scrooge. "A remarkable boy! Do you know whether they've sold the prize turkey that was hanging up there?—not the little prize turkey—the big one?"

"What, the one as big as me?" returned the boy.

"What a delightful boy!" said Scrooge. "It's a pleasure to talk to him. Yes, my buck!"

"It's hanging there now," replied the boy.

"Is it?" said Scrooge. "Go and buy it."

"Walk-er!" exclaimed the boy.

"No, no," said Scrooge, "I am in earnest. Go and buy it, and tell 'em to bring it here, that I may give them the direction where to take it. Come back with the man and I'll give you a shilling. Come back with him in less than five minutes and I'll give you half-a-crown!"

The boy was off like a shot. He must have had a steady hand at a trigger who could have got a shot off half so fast.

"I'll send it to Bob Cratchit's!" whispered Scrooge, rubbing his hands and splitting with a laugh. "He sha'n't know who sends it. It's twice the size of Tiny Tim. Joe Miller never made such a joke as sending it to Bob's will be!"

The hand in which he wrote the address was not a steady one, but write it he did, somehow, and went downstairs to open the street door, ready for the coming of the poulterer's man. As he stood there waiting his arrival, the knocker caught his eye.

"I shall love it as long as I live!" cried Scrooge, patting it with his hand. "I scarcely ever looked at it before. What an honest expression it has in its face! It's a wonderful knocker! Here's the turkey. Hallo! Whoop! How are you! Merry Christmas!"

It *was* a turkey! He never could have stood upon his legs, that bird. He would have snapped 'em short off in a minute, like sticks of sealing wax.

"Why, it's impossible to carry that to Camden Town," said Scrooge. "You must have a cab."

The chuckle with which he said this, and the chuckle with which he paid for the turkey, and the chuckle with which he paid for the cab, and the chuckle with which he recompensed the boy, were only to be exceeded by the chuckle with which he sat down breathless in his chair again, and chuckled till he cried.

Shaving was not an easy task, for his hand continued to shake very much, and shaving requires attention, even when you don't dance while you are at it. But if he had cut the end of his nose off, he would have put a piece of sticking-plaster over it, and been quite satisfied.

He dressed himself "all in his best," and at last got out into the streets. The people were by this time pouring forth, as he had seen them with the Ghost of Christmas Present, and walking with his hands behind him, Scrooge regarded every one with a delighted smile. He looked so irresistibly pleasant, in a word, that three or four good-humored fellows said, "Good morning, sir! A merry Christmas to you!" And Scrooge said often afterwards, that of all the blithe sounds he had ever heard, those were the blithest in his ears.

He had not gone far, when coming on towards him he beheld a portly gentleman who had walked into his counting-house the day before and said, "Scrooge and Marley's I believe?" It sent a pang across his heart to think how this old gentleman would look upon him when they met, but he knew what path lay straight before him, and he took it.

"My dear sir," said Scrooge, quickening his pace, and taking the old gentleman by both his hands, "how do you do? I hope you succeeded yesterday. It was very kind of you. A merry Christmas to you, sir!"

"Mr. Scrooge?"

"Yes," said Scrooge, "that is my name, and I fear it may not be pleasant to you. Allow me to ask your pardon. And will you have the goodness"—here Scrooge whispered in his ear.

"Lord bless me!" cried the gentleman, as if his breath was taken away. "My dear Mr. Scrooge, are you serious?"

"If you please," said Scrooge. "Not a farthing less. A great many back payments are included in it, I assure you. Will you do me that favor?"

"My dear sir," said the other, shaking hands with him, "I don't know what to say to such munifi—"

"Don't say anything, please," retorted Scrooge. "Come and see me. Will you come and see me?"

"I will!" cried the old gentleman. And it was clear that he meant to do it.

"Thank'ee," said Scrooge. "I am much obliged to you. I thank you fifty times. Bless you!"

He went to church, and walked about the streets, and watched the people hurrying to and fro, and patted children on the head, and questioned beggars, and looked down into the kitchens of houses, and up to the windows, and found that everything could yield him pleasure. He had never dreamed that any walk—that anything—could give him so much happiness. In the afternoon he turned his steps towards his nephew's house.

He passed the door a dozen times before he had the courage to go up and knock; but he made a dash, and did it.

"Is your master at home, my dear?" said Scrooge to the girl. Nice girl! Very.

"Yes, sir."

"Where is he, my love?" said Scrooge.

"He's in the dining-room, sir, along with mistress. I'll show you upstairs, if you please."

"Thank'ee. He knows me," said Scrooge, with his hand already on the dining-room lock. "I'll go in here, my dear."

He turned it gently, and sidled his face in, round the door. They were looking at the table (which was spread out in great array), for these young housekeepers are always nervous on such points, and like to see that everything is right.

"Fred!" said Scrooge.

Dear heart alive, how his niece by marriage started! Scrooge had forgotten, for the moment, about her sitting in the corner with the footstool, or he wouldn't have done it on any account.

"Why, bless my soul!" cried Fred, "who's that?"

"It's I. Your Uncle Scrooge. I have come to dinner. Will you let me in, Fred?"

Let him in! It is a mercy he didn't shake his arm off. He was at home in five minutes. Nothing could be heartier. His niece looked just the same. So did Topper when *he* came. So did the plump sister when *she* came. So did every one when *they* came. Wonderful party, wonderful games, wonderful unanimity, wonderful happiness!

But he was early at the office next morning. Oh, he was early there. If he could only be there first, and catch Bob Cratchit coming late! That was the thing he had set his heart upon.

And he did it; yes, he did! The clock struck nine. No Bob. A quarter past. No Bob. He was full eighteen minutes and a half behind his time. Scrooge sat with his door wide open, that he might see him come into the tank.

His hat was off before he opened the door; his comforter, too. He was on his stool in a jiffy, driving away with his pen, as if he were trying to overtake nine o'clock.

"Hallo!" growled Scrooge, in his accustomed voice, as near as he could feign it. "What do you mean by coming here at this time of day?"

"I'm very sorry, sir," said Bob. "I *am* behind my time."

"You are?" repeated Scrooge. "Yes, I think you are. Step this way, sir, if you please."

"It's only once a year, sir," pleaded Bob, appearing from the tank. "It shall not be repeated. I was making rather merry yesterday, sir."

"Now, I'll tell you what, my friend," said Scrooge, "I am not going to stand this sort of thing any longer. And therefore," he continued, leaping from his stool, and giving Bob such a dig in the waistcoat that he staggered back into the tank again, "and therefore I am about to raise your salary!"

Bob trembled, and got a little nearer to the ruler. He had a momentary idea of knocking Scrooge down with it, holding him, and calling to the people in the court for help and a straight-waistcoat.

"A Merry Christmas, Bob!" said Scrooge, with an earnestness that could not be mistaken, as he clapped him on the back. "A merrier Christmas, Bob, my good fellow, than I have given you for many a year! I'll raise your salary, and endeavor to assist your struggling family, and we will discuss your affairs this very afternoon over a Christmas bowl of smoking bishop, Bob! Make up the fires and buy another coal-scuttle before you dot another i, Bob Cratchit!"

Scrooge was better than his word. He did it all, and infinitely more; and to Tiny Tim, who did *not* die, he was a second father. He became as good a friend, as good a master, and as good a man as the good old city knew, or any other good old city, town, or borough in the good old world. Some people laughed to see the alteration in him, but he let them laugh, and little heeded them, for he was wise enough to know that nothing ever happened on this globe, for good, at which some people did not have their fill of laughter in the outset, and knowing that such as these would be blind anyway, he thought it quite as well that they should wrinkle up their eyes in grins, as have the malady in less attractive forms. His own heart laughed, and that was quite enough for him.

He had no further intercourse with Spirits, but lived upon the Total Abstinence Principle ever afterwards, and it was always said of him, that he knew how to keep Christmas well, if any man alive possessed the knowledge. May that be truly said of us, and all of us! And so, as Tiny Tim observed, God bless us, every one!

VII.

LITTLE GRETCHEN AND THE WOODEN SHOE.

A CHRISTMAS STORY FOR LITTLE CHILDREN.

The following story is one of many which has drifted down to us from the story-loving nurseries and hearthstones of Germany. I cannot recall when I first had it told to me as a child, varied of course by different tellers, but always leaving that sweet, tender impression of God's loving care for the least of his children. I have since read different versions of it in at least a half-dozen story books for children.

Once upon a time, a long time ago, far away across the great ocean, in a country called Germany, there could be seen a small log hut on the edge of a great forest, whose fir-trees extended for miles and miles to the north. This little house, made of heavy hewn logs, had but one room in it. A rough pine door gave entrance to this room, and a small square window admitted the light. At the back of the house was built an old-fashioned stone chimney, out of which in winter usually curled a thin blue smoke, showing that there was not very much fire within.

Small as the house was, it was large enough for the two people who lived in it. I want to tell you a story to-day about these two people. One was an old, gray-haired woman, so old that the little children of the village, nearly half a mile away, often wondered whether she had come into the world with the huge mountains and the great fir-trees, which stood like giants back of her small hut. Her face was wrinkled all over with deep lines, which if the children could only have read aright, would have told them of many years of cheerful, happy, self-sacrifice, of loving, anxious watching beside sick-beds, of quiet endurance of pain, of many a day of hunger and cold, and of a thousand deeds of unselfish love for other people; but, of course, they could not read this strange handwriting. They only knew that she was old and wrinkled, and that she stooped as she walked. None of them seemed to fear her, for her smile was always cheerful, and she had a kindly word for each of them if they chanced to meet her on her way to and from the village. With this old, old woman lived a very little girl. So bright and happy was she that the travelers who passed by the lonesome little house on the edge of the forest often thought of a sunbeam as they saw her. These two people were known in the village as Granny Goodyear and Little Gretchen.

The winter had come and the frost had snapped off many of the smaller branches from the pine-trees in the forest. Gretchen and her Granny were up by daybreak each morning. After their simple breakfast of oatmeal, Gretchen would run to the little closet and fetch Granny's old woolen shawl, which seemed almost as old as Granny herself. Gretchen always claimed the right to put the shawl over her Granny's head, even though she had to climb onto the wooden bench to do it. After carefully pinning it under Granny's chin, she gave her a good by kiss, and Granny started out for her morning's work in the forest. This work was nothing more nor less than the gathering up of the twigs and branches which the autumn winds and winter frosts had thrown upon the ground. These were carefully gathered into a large bundle which Granny tied together with a strong linen band. She then managed to lift the bundle to her shoulder and trudged off to the village with it. Here she sold the fagots for kindling wood to the people of the village. Sometimes she would get only a few pence each day, and sometimes a dozen or more, but on this money little Gretchen and she managed to live; they had their home, and the forest kindly furnished the wood for the fire which kept them warm in cold weather.

In the summer-time Granny had a little garden at the back of the hut where she raised, with little Gretchen's help, a few potatoes and turnips and onions. These she carefully stored away for winter use. To this meager supply, the pennies, gained by selling the twigs from the forest, added the oatmeal for Gretchen and a little black coffee for Granny. Meat was a thing they never thought of having. It cost too much money. Still, Granny and Gretchen were very happy, because they loved each other dearly.

Sometimes Gretchen would be left alone all day long in the hut because Granny would have some work to do in the village after selling her bundle of sticks and twigs. It was during these long days that little Gretchen had taught herself to sing the song which the wind sang to the pine branches. In the summer-time she learned the chirp and twitter of the birds, until her voice might almost be mistaken for a bird's voice; she learned to dance as the swaying shadows did, and even to talk to the stars which shone through the little square window when Granny came home too late or too tired to talk.

Sometimes when the weather was fine, or her Granny had an extra bundle of newly knitted stockings to take to the village, she would let little Gretchen go along with her. It chanced that one of these trips to the town came just the week before Christmas, and Gretchen's eyes were delighted by the sight of the lovely Christmas trees which stood in the window of the village store. It seemed to her that she would never tire of looking at the knit dolls, the woolly lambs, the little wooden shops with their queer, painted men and women in them, and all the other fine things. She had never owned a play-thing in her whole life; therefore, toys which you and I would not think much of, seemed to her to be very beautiful.

That night, after their supper of baked potatoes was over, and little Gretchen had cleared away the dishes and swept up the hearth because Granny dear was so tired, she brought her own small wooden stool and placed it very near Granny's feet and sat down upon it, folding her hands on her lap. Granny knew that this meant she wanted to talk about something, so she smilingly laid away the large Bible which she had been reading, and took up her knitting, which was as much as to say: "Well, Gretchen, dear, Granny is ready to listen."

"Granny," said Gretchen slowly, "it's almost Christmas time, isn't it?"

"Yes, dearie," said Granny, "only five more days now," and then she sighed, but little Gretchen was so happy that she did not notice Granny's sigh.

"What do you think, Granny, I'll get this Christmas?" said she, looking up eagerly into Granny's face.

"Ah, child, child," said Granny, shaking her head, "you'll have no Christmas this year. We are too poor for that."

"Oh, but Granny," interrupted little Gretchen, "think of all the beautiful toys we saw in the village to-day. Surely Santa Claus has sent enough for every little child."

"Ah, dearie," said Granny, "those toys are for people who can pay money for them, and we have no money to spend for Christmas toys."

"Well, Granny," said Gretchen, "perhaps some of the little children who live in the great house on the hill at the other end of the village will be willing to share some of their toys with me. They will be so glad to give some to a little girl who has none."

"Dear child, dear child," said Granny, leaning forward and stroking the soft, shiny hair of the little girl, "your heart is full of love. You would be glad to bring a Christmas to every child; but their heads are so full of what they are going to get that they forget all about anybody else but themselves." Then she sighed and shook her head.

"Well, Granny," said Gretchen, her bright, happy tone of voice growing a little less joyous, "perhaps the dear Santa Claus will show some of the village children how to make presents that do not cost money, and some of them may surprise me Christmas morning with a present. And, Granny, dear," added she, springing up from her low stool, "can't I gather some of the pine branches and take them to the old sick man who lives in the house by the mill, so that he can have the sweet smell of our pine forest in his room all Christmas day?"

"Yes, dearie," said Granny, "you may do what you can to make the Christmas bright and happy, but you must not expect any present yourself."

"Oh, but Granny," said little Gretchen, her face brightening, "you forget all about the shining Christmas angels, who came down to earth and sang their wonderful song the night the beautiful Christ Child was born! They are so loving and good that *they* will not forget any little child. I shall ask my dear stars to-night to tell them of us. You know," she added, with a look of relief, "the stars are so very high that they must know the angels quite well, as they come and go with their messages from the loving God."

Granny sighed, as she half whispered, "Poor child, poor child!" but Gretchen threw her arm around Granny's neck and gave her a hearty kiss, saying as she did so: "Oh, Granny, Granny, you don't talk to the stars often enough, else you wouldn't be sad at Christmas time." Then she danced all around the room, whirling her little skirts about her to show Granny how the wind had made the snow dance that day. She looked so droll and funny that Granny forgot her cares and worries and laughed with little Gretchen over her new snow-dance. The days passed on, and the morning before Christmas Eve came. Gretchen having tidied up the little room—for Granny had taught her to be a careful housewife—was off to the forest, singing a bird-like song, almost as happy and free as the birds themselves. She was very busy that day, preparing a surprise for Granny. First, however, she gathered the most beautiful of the fir branches within her reach to take the next morning to the old sick man who lived by the mill.

The day was all too short for the happy little girl. When Granny came trudging wearily home that night, she found the frame of the doorway covered with green pine branches.

"It's to welcome you, Granny! It's to welcome you!" cried Gretchen; "our dear old home wanted to give you a Christmas welcome. Don't you see, the branches of evergreen make it look as if it were smiling all over, and it is trying to say, 'A happy Christmas' to you, Granny!"

Granny laughed and kissed the little girl, as they opened the door and went in together. Here was a new surprise for Granny. The four posts of the wooden bed, which stood in one corner of the room, had been trimmed by the busy little fingers with smaller and more flexible branches of the pine-trees. A small bouquet of red mountain-ash berries stood at each side of the fireplace, and these, together with the trimmed posts of the bed, gave the plain old room quite a festival look. Gretchen laughed and clapped her hands and danced about until the house seemed full of music to poor, tired Granny, whose heart had been sad as she turned towards their home that night, thinking of the disappointment which must come to loving little Gretchen the next morning.

After supper was over little Gretchen drew her stool up to Granny's side, and laying her soft, little hands on Granny's knee, asked to be told once again the story of the coming of the Christ Child; how the night that he was born the beautiful angels had sung their wonderful song, and how the whole sky had become bright with a strange and glorious light, never seen by the people of earth before. Gretchen had heard the story many, many times before, but she never grew tired of it, and now that Christmas Eve had come again, the happy little child wanted to hear it once more.

When Granny had finished telling it the two sat quiet and silent for a little while thinking it over; then Granny rose and said that it was time for them to go to bed. She slowly took off her heavy wooden shoes, such as are worn in that country, and placed them beside the hearth. Gretchen looked thoughtfully at them for a minute or two, and then she said, "Granny, don't you think that *somebody* in all this wide world will think of us to-night?"

"Nay, Gretchen," said Granny, "I don't think any one will."

"Well, then, Granny," said Gretchen, "the Christmas angels will, I know; so I am going to take one of your wooden shoes, and put it on the window sill outside, so that they may see it as they pass by. I am sure the stars will tell the Christmas angels where the shoe is."

"Ah, you foolish, foolish child," said Granny; "you are only getting ready for a disappointment. To-morrow morning there will be nothing whatever in the shoe. I can tell you that now."

But little Gretchen would not listen. She only shook her head and cried out: "Ah, Granny, you don't talk enough to the stars." With this she seized the shoe, and opening the door, hurried out to place it on the window-sill. It was very dark without, and something soft and cold seemed to gently kiss her hair and face. Gretchen knew by this that it was snowing, and she looked up to the sky, anxious to see if the stars were in sight, but a strong wind was tumbling the dark, heavy snow-clouds about and had shut away all else.

"Never mind," said Gretchen softly to herself, "the stars are up there, even if I can't see them, and the Christmas angels do not mind snow-storms."

Just then a rough wind went sweeping by the little girl, whispering something to her which she could not understand, and then it made a sudden rush up to the snow-clouds and parted them, so that the deep, mysterious sky appeared beyond, and shining down out of the midst of it was Gretchen's favorite star.

"Ah, little star, little star!" said the child, laughing aloud, "I knew you were there, though I couldn't see you. Will you whisper to the Christmas angels as they come by, that little Gretchen wants so very much to have a Christmas gift to-morrow morning if they have one to spare, and that she has put one of Granny's shoes upon the window-sill ready for it?"

A moment more and the little girl, standing on tiptoe, had reached the window-sill and placed the shoe upon it, and was back in the house again beside Granny and the warm fire. The two went quietly to bed, and that night as little Gretchen knelt to pray to the Heavenly Father, she thanked him for having sent the Christ Child into the world to teach all mankind how to be loving and unselfish, and in a few moments she was quietly sleeping, dreaming of the Christmas angels.

The next morning, very early, even before the sun was up, little Gretchen was awakened by the sound of sweet music coming from the village. She listened for a moment and then she knew that the choir-boys were singing the Christmas carols in the open air of the village street. She sprang out of bed and began to dress herself as quickly as possible, singing as she dressed. While Granny was slowly putting on her clothes, little Gretchen, having finished dressing herself, unfastened the door and hurried out to see what the Christmas angels had left in the old wooden shoe.

The white snow covered everything—trees, stumps, roads, and pastures—until the whole world looked like fairyland. Gretchen climbed up on a large stone which was beneath the window and carefully lifted down the wooden shoe. The snow tumbled off of it in a shower over the little girl's hands, but she did not heed that; she ran hurriedly back into the house, putting her hand into the toe of the shoe as she ran.

"Oh, Granny! Oh, Granny!" she exclaimed, "you didn't believe the Christmas angels would think about us, but see, they have, they have! Here is a dear little bird nestled down in the toe of your shoe! Oh, isn't he beautiful!"

Granny came forward and looked at what the child was holding lovingly in her hand. There she saw a tiny chick-a-dee, whose wing was evidently broken by the rough and boisterous winds of the night before, and who had taken shelter in the safe, dry toe of the old wooden shoe. She gently took the little bird out of Gretchen's hands, and skilfully bound his broken wing to his side, so that he need not hurt himself by trying to fly with it. Then she showed Gretchen how to make a nice warm nest for the little stranger, close beside the fire, and when their breakfast was ready she let Gretchen feed the little bird with a few moist crumbs.

Later in the day Gretchen carried the fresh, green boughs to the old sick man by the mill, and on her way home stopped to see and enjoy the Christmas toys of some other children whom she knew, never once wishing that they were hers. When she reached home she found that the little bird had gone to sleep. Soon, however, he opened his eyes and stretched his head up, saying just as plain as a bird could say, "Now, my new friends, I want you to give me something more to eat." Gretchen gladly fed him again, and then holding him in her lap, she softly and gently stroked his gray feathers until the little creature seemed to lose all fear of her. That evening Granny taught her a Christmas hymn and told her another beautiful Christmas story. Then Gretchen made up a funny little story to tell to the birdie. He winked his eyes and turned his head from side to side in such a droll fashion that Gretchen laughed until the tears came.

As Granny and she got ready for bed that night, Gretchen put her arms softly around Granny's neck, and whispered: "What a beautiful Christmas we have had to-day, Granny! Is there anything in the world more lovely than Christmas?"

"Nay, child, nay," said Granny, "not to such loving hearts as yours."

VIII.

THE LEGEND OF THE CHRIST CHILD. [3]

A STORY FOR CHRISTMAS EVE.

I want to tell you to-night a story which has been told to little children in Germany for many hundreds of years.

Once upon a time, a long, long time ago, on the night before Christmas, a little child was wandering all alone through the streets of a great city. There were many people on the street, fathers and mothers, sisters and brothers, uncles and aunts, and even gray-haired grandfathers and grandmothers, all of whom were hurrying home with bundles of presents for each other and for their little ones. Fine carriages rolled by, express wagons rattled past, even old carts were pressed into service, and all things seemed in a hurry, and glad with expectation of the coming Christmas morning.

From some of the windows bright lights were already beginning to stream until it was almost as bright as day. But the little child seemed to have no home, and wandered about listlessly from street to street. No one took any notice of him, except perhaps Jack Frost, who bit his bare toes and made the ends of his fingers tingle. The north wind, too, seemed to notice the child, for it blew against him and pierced his ragged garments through and through, causing him to shiver with cold. Home after home he passed, looking with longing eyes through the windows, in upon the glad, happy children, most of whom were helping to trim the Christmas trees for the coming morrow.

"Surely," said the child to himself, "where there is so much gladness and happiness, some of it may be for me." So with timid steps he approached a large and handsome house. Through the windows he could see a tall and stately Christmas tree already lighted. Many presents hung upon it. Its green boughs were trimmed with gold and silver ornaments. Slowly he climbed up the broad steps and gently rapped at the door. It was opened by a large man-servant. He had a kindly face, although his voice was deep and gruff. He looked at the little child for a moment, then sadly shook his head and said, "Go down off the steps. There is no room here for such as you." He looked sorry as he spoke; possibly he remembered his own little ones at home, and was glad that they were not out in this cold and bitter night. Through the open door a bright light shone, and the warm air, filled with the fragrance of the Christmas pine, rushed out from the inner room and greeted the little wanderer with a kiss. As the child turned back into the cold and darkness, he wondered why the footman had spoken thus, for surely, thought he, those little children would love to have another companion join them in their joyous Christmas festival. But the little children inside did not even know that he had knocked at the door.

The street grew colder and darker as the child passed on. He went sadly forward, saying to himself, "Is there no one in all this great city who will share the Christmas with me?" Farther and farther down the street he wandered, to where the homes were not so large and beautiful. There seemed to be little children inside of nearly all the houses. They were dancing and frolicking about. Christmas trees could be seen in nearly every window, with beautiful dolls and trumpets and picture-books and balls and tops and other dainty toys hung upon them. In one window the child noticed a little lamb made of soft, white wool. Around its neck was tied a red ribbon. It had evidently been hung on the tree for one of the children. The little stranger stopped before this window and looked long and earnestly at the beautiful things inside, but most of all was he drawn toward the white lamb. At last, creeping up to the window-pane, he gently tapped upon it. A little girl came to the window and looked out into the dark street where the snow had now begun to fall. She saw the child, but she only frowned and shook her head and said, "Go away and come some other time. We are too busy to take care of you now." Back into the dark, cold street he turned again. The wind was whirling past him and seemed to say, "Hurry on, hurry on, we have no time to stop. 'Tis Christmas Eve and everybody is in a hurry to-night."

Again and again the little child rapped softly at door or window-pane. At each place he was refused admission. One mother feared he might have some ugly disease which her darlings would catch; another father said he had only enough for his own children, and none to spare for beggar brats. Still another told him to go home where he belonged, and not to trouble other folks.

The hours passed; later grew the night, and colder blew the wind, and darker seemed the street. Farther and farther the little one wandered. There was scarcely any one left upon the street by this time, and the few who remained did not seem to see the child, when suddenly ahead of him, there appeared a bright, single ray of light. It shone through the darkness into the child's eyes. He looked up smilingly, and said, "I will go where the small light beckons, perhaps they will share their Christmas with me."

Hurrying past all the other houses he soon reached the end of the street and went straight up to the window from which the light was streaming. It was a poor, little, low house, but the child cared not for that. The light seemed still to call him in. From what do you suppose the light came? Nothing but a tallow candle which had been placed in an old cup with a broken handle, in the window, as a glad token of Christmas Eve. There was neither curtain nor shade to the small, square window, and as the little child looked in he saw standing upon a neat, wooden table a branch of a Christmas tree. The room was plainly furnished, but it was very clean. Near the fireplace sat a lovely faced mother with a little two-year-old on her knee and an older child beside her. The two children were looking into their mother's face and listening to a story. She must have been telling them a Christmas story, I think. A few bright coals were burning in the fireplace, and all seemed light and warm within.

The little wanderer crept closer and closer to the window-pane. So sweet was the mother's face, so loving seemed the little children, that at last he took courage and tapped gently, very gently, on the door. The mother stopped talking, the little children looked up. "What was that, mother?" asked the little girl at her side. "I think it was some one tapping on the door," replied the mother. "Run as quickly as you can and open it, dear, for it is a bitter cold night to keep any one waiting in this storm." "Oh, mother, I think it was the bough of the tree tapping against the window-pane," said the little girl. "Do please go on with our story." Again the little wanderer tapped upon the door. "My child! my child," exclaimed the mother, rising, "that certainly was a rap on the door. Run quickly and open it. No one must be left out in the cold on our beautiful Christmas Eve."

The child ran to the door and threw it wide open. The mother saw the ragged stranger standing without, cold and shivering, with bare head and almost bare feet. She held out both hands and drew him into the warm, bright room. "You poor dear child," was all she said, and putting her arms around him, she drew him close to her breast. "He is very cold, my children," she exclaimed. "We must warm him." "And," added the little girl, "we must love him and give him some of our Christmas, too." "Yes," said the mother, "but first let us warm him."

The mother sat down beside the fire with the child on her lap, and her own two little ones warmed his half-frozen hands in theirs. The mother smoothed his tangled curls, and bending low over his head, kissed the child's face. She gathered the three little ones in her arms and the candle and the fire light shone over them. For a moment the room was very still. By and by the little girl said, softly, to her mother, "May we not light the Christmas tree, and let him see how beautiful it looks?" "Yes," said the mother. With that she seated the child on a low stool beside the fire, and went herself to fetch the few simple ornaments which from year to year she had saved for her children's Christmas tree. They were soon so busy that they did not notice the room had filled with a strange and brilliant light. They turned and looked at the spot where the little wanderer sat. His ragged clothes had changed to garments white and beautiful; his tangled curls seemed like a halo of golden light about his head; but most glorious of all was his face, which shone with a light so dazzling that they could scarcely look upon it.

In silent wonder they gazed at the child. Their little room seemed to grow larger and larger until it was as wide as the whole world, the roof of their low house seemed to expand and rise, until it reached to the sky.

With a sweet and gentle smile the wonderful child looked upon them for a moment, and then slowly rose and floated through the air, above the treetops, beyond the church spire, higher even than the clouds themselves, until he appeared to them to be a shining star in the sky above. At last he disappeared from sight. The astonished children turned in hushed awe to their mother, and said, in a whisper, "Oh, mother, it was the Christ Child, was it not?" And the mother answered in a low tone, "Yes."

And it is said, dear children, that each Christmas Eve the little Christ Child wanders through some town or village, and those who receive him and take him into their homes and hearts have given to them this marvelous vision which is denied to others.

www.ingramcontent.com/pod-product-compliance
Lightning Source LLC
Chambersburg PA
CBHW080909190726
48294CB00008B/2018